The Girl with Nine Wigs

Sophie van der Stap

Om Books International

Sophie van der Stap was 21 years-old when she was diagnosed with a rare form of cancer. A striking, fun-loving student, overnight her world was reduced to the sterile confines of a hospital. But within these walls Sophie discovered a whole new world of white coats, gossiping nurses, and sexy doctors. Of shared rooms, hair loss, and eyebrow pencils.

Sophie wrote of her experiences in her refreshingly candid book, *The Girl with Nine Wigs*. When it was originally published in The Netherlands in 2006, it became an instant bestseller and won the Bart Prize for "Making the Impossible Possible." It also stormed the charts internationally. The Academy Award-winning producer Andreas Bareiss is currently adapting *The Girl with Nine Wigs* into a film.

In 2011, Sophie released a novel, *And What if This Were Love*, telling the story of a blind woman, Madame de Grenelle, hiding from herself. After two years of intensive writing (columns and essays) for Dutch newspapers *NRC Next* and *NRC Handelsblad*, she's currently working on two novels.

Sophie is now 32 years-old and has lives for many years in Paris. Her cancer is in complete remission. She still occasionally wears wigs.

First published in 2016 by

Om Books International

Corporate & Editorial Office
A-12, Sector 64, Noida 201 301
Uttar Pradesh, India
Phone: +91 120 477 4100
Email: editorial@ombooks.com
Website: www.ombooksinternational.com

Sales Office
107, Ansari Road, Darya Ganj,
New Delhi 110 002, India
Phone: +91 11 4000 9000
Fax: +91 11 2327 8091
Email: sales@ombooks.com
Website: www.ombooks.com

ISBN: 978-93-85609-40-4

Printed in India

10 9 8 7 6 5 4 3 2 1

As you set out for Ithaka
hope your road is a long one,
full of adventure, full of discovery.

—*C. P. Cavafy*

THURSDAY, JANUARY 13

Before, my daily routine was to wake up at eight for a long run in the park, then have my coffee while rushing off to class. Now I wake up with a cough, and I'm lucky if I can run half the distance in double the time. Lately I need three coffees just to get going, and I still end up being late for class.

Visiting the hospital is a thrilling part of my new routine. After numerous appointments with multiple doctors in various hospitals and two visits to the emergency room, I now find myself in yet another antiseptic hospital lounge with stale magazines, waiting to see a new doctor with a new diagnosis and a new file.

At this point, I know this hospital like the back of my hand. I've spent the past two months wandering from one department to the next, from the top floor to the bottom, from the front to the back. Over and over and over again. I've seen eight interns, two gynecologists—why do doctors always assume you're pregnant when they can't figure out what's wrong?—a pulmonary specialist, and two ER teams, and have been prescribed three courses of antibiotics. All to no avail. Between all these doctors, no diagnosis but plenty of symptoms and a lost tampon. Ick. It gave the doctors and my father, who was waiting in the hallway, a big laugh but left me mortified.

My symptoms—a strange jabbing here and there, shortness of breath, the loss of a few kilos (which I'm definitely not complaining about), and a pale face that no amount of blush can mask—don't seem to bring me to a diagnosis. So here I am in the waiting room. Again. A door opens and I see him—the one hundredth white coat to examine me and try to figure out what is causing all these seemingly unrelated symptoms. He approaches the reception desk, picks up my file, and calls out "Miss van der Stap" while randomly scanning the waiting room to see which of the rumpled contestants has just won a spot in his examination room. He calmly acknowledges me as I stand up. *A teenager.* I can practically see the thought forming in his mind as he looks at me. But he touches my dream: handsome face, nice hands, fortysomething. Finally, my *Grey's Anatomy* fantasy is becoming a reality. Who knew that a hospital would turn out to be a great place for a single girl like me? I abandon my mom in the waiting room and follow him, gingerly, down the hall.

As my details are taken down for what feels like the hundredth time—amid all these technologically advanced supermachines, they still can't keep track of my records—I take advantage of this time and study Dr. McDreamy more closely. His nametag says DR. K, PULMONARY SPECIALIST. *I'm guessing early forties. Charming, handsome, and smart: a playboy or happily married in the suburbs? Or maybe both? Better Google him later. A white coat can be misleading, but shoes never lie. Brogues, black leather. Hmm ... Not bad, not great either.* Not much to go on, but given his age I decide to give him the benefit of the doubt.

He tells me to take a seat and asks me to lift up my top. I'm allowed to keep on my bra. He places a cold metal stethoscope against my chest, and then on my back.

He listens, I sigh.

I sigh, he listens.

I listen, he sighs.

"Something isn't quite right," he says. His words don't scare me. In fact, I'm even a bit relieved. It's been blatantly clear for a long time that something's wrong; finally, someone else is catching on. Handsome *and* smart. Dr. K might be the answer to this Kafkaesque hospital. At last I'll get a diagnosis and some pills in a jar. Back to normal life.

He finishes examining me but wants me to get my lungs X-rayed on the first floor and then come back and see him. Later, when I get back to Dr. K, pictures of my lungs in hand, he leads me to a different room, where I sit perched on an exam table, the words ENDOSCOPY AND PULMONARY RESEARCH hanging above my head.

"These X-rays don't look good," he says. "There's fluid in your right lung that we need to drain."

"Drain?"

"Yes, via a tube in your back."

I swallow. I'm not sure what this tube means, but it doesn't sound like something I want stuck in my back.

This time the bra doesn't stay on. I feel exposed. I'm uncomfortable, and I'm suddenly starting to feel scared and out of place. *Why are there all these people fussing over me all of a sudden?* I feel outnumbered and wish I hadn't told my mom to wait outside, but I'm too proud to change my mind now. So I sit there shivering as Dr. K, his assistant, whose choice of footwear clearly states that she's more into me than into my doctor, and a clean-shaven intern named Floris prepare a monstrous needle. Three sets of eyes are directed at my two little mounds. *Or maybe they're too busy looking at the horrible needle that is about to be stuck into my back and straight through to my lung?* Floris seems just as uncomfortable as I am and avoids looking at me directly, which makes the awkwardness I'm feeling grow even more palpable in the small room.

Dr. K's assistant begins to explain to me what is about to happen and why they think it's necessary to puncture my insides: "The X-rays show that there is about three-quarters of a liter of fluid between your lung and your pleura, the sac surrounding your lungs."

"Oh."

"If it's yellow pus, that's bad news," she continues. "That means there's an infection."

"Oh."

"It's better if it's clear fluid."

"Oh."

She gives me a shot of anesthetic to numb my back, but I wish she had given me two. I feel every excruciating inch of that tube as it's being pushed through my back. Dr. K immediately comes to my rescue with a second shot of anesthetic when he sees me wince with pain. The tube is long enough for me to see the fluid streaming from my back. The fluid isn't yellow, but, as it turns out, what it is isn't great either.

Dr. K asks me for my cell phone number. I'm flattered: everybody knows that cell phone numbers are for dating, not for doctors. The next evening he calls while I'm having dinner with my parents.

"I can't figure out exactly what's going on. I want to admit you for a week so we can run a number of tests. We'll start with an endoscopy."

"An endosco-what?"

"We'll make a small incision about two centimeters long on the side of your back and go inside with a tiny camera to take a closer look at your lungs. While we're in there we'll take some tissue samples as well."

"Oh ... sure, if you think it's necessary." I hang up the phone as the first tears come. Suddenly it hits me that this might actually be the start of a long-term relationship with Dr. K, only not in the way I'd hoped. I wipe away my tears before returning to the table. "The doctor just likes having me around," I joke to my parents, who laugh along briefly. We finish the rest of the meal in strained silence.

* * *

Dr. K doesn't waste any time. The next thing I know, instead of staring at the tapestries on my bedroom walls or the souvenirs from far-off places that fill the room, I'm looking at the sterile walls of the hospital.

For a week I lay there in my white room, in my white bed, in my white hospital gown, surrounded by white, white, white. Everywhere I look there are white nurses' uniforms, white gauze, and white lights shining down that give everyone a chalky pallor. Even the doctors and nurses look sick. I have a tube down my nose, a collapsed lung from the endoscopy, and a respirator hanging above my head. There's a lot going on and none of it is good; none of it seems to be leading to any answers. The only silver lining is that I'm finally getting around to some heavy reading. You know, those books you always swear you're going to read but somehow never have time for? Dr. K—whom I've cast as a leading role in my fantasies—comes to visit me every day to see how Anna

Karenina and I are getting along. *Well, at least I'm doing better than she is.*

After a week of hospital tests and scans, they release me on Friday night, just in time for the next semester of university to begin.

MONDAY, JANUARY 24

But instead of going back to university, on Monday my father and I are once again sitting in an office of the hospital, and this time opposite a much less handsome face. I try to hide my disappointment as he informs us that Dr. K is at a conference for the week. Whatever, at least somebody will finally be giving me a diagnosis. Suddenly I understand that we've all been worried, but nobody has been talking about it out loud. I think my family is afraid that sharing our worries will make them real, and there's been enough fear recently; my mother just finished her last chemotherapy. She was diagnosed with breast cancer about a year ago. At home, the champagne is on ice. Soon we'll be on our way, diagnosis in hand, which for us, after all we've been through, is as good as a cure.

"We received the results from the lab. It's not good. It's cancer."

For a moment I just sit there, my mouth wide open. Then my eyes fill with tears and all the strength drains out of me as I collapse on the floor. I crawl under the desk to hide—maybe cancer doesn't exist under desks. The moment is at once completely surreal and terrifyingly real.

At some point I remember that my father is there. I look up at him—he's just staring off into the distance. My first instinct is to comfort him, but words fail me. I can see the tears reflected in his glasses. He's trying desperately to fight them back, probably thinking the same thing I am: Mom just won her own battle with breast cancer. She went through chemo only two doors down from where we're sitting. It can't be happening again. Not to me. Not when I'm only twenty-one.

Eventually my legs start to work again. I get out from under the desk and hide myself in my thick down coat, looking for some kind of physical comfort. But it just keeps getting colder. I want to leave. I want to run away so that the last few minutes of my life can be erased. No one except my father and me know that this nightmare is happening. It hasn't yet entered the lives of those around us, and if I run fast to them now, maybe it won't exist in mine either. I turn my back to leave. The doctor asks me where I am going. *Who the hell knows?* The only thing I know is that I have to get out of here. Away from him. I instantly hate this man. Where the hell is Dr. K? Not only is this creature sitting behind my beloved Dr. K's desk with his arms crossed, now he's telling me I have cancer!

I'm not supposed to be here, at the hospital. I'm supposed to be at my first day of classes for the semester. Outside, students are running to make it to their lectures, coffee in one hand and newspaper in the other. Outside, in our home, my mother and sister are waiting for a reason to pop the champagne.

But inside, I have cancer. We are sent to the oncology ward: Cancer HQ. There the nightmare is confirmed and the truth begins to sink in for real. I'm no longer in the pulmonary department, no longer under Dr. K's care. I sit there, comatose, as my new doctor, Dr. L, discusses my body's malfunctioning as if he were a mechanic. *Gross.* His first words are a blur; all I hear is "aggressive," "advanced," and "rare." "Rhabdomyosarcoma," he calls it.

"The cancer reaches from the lungs down to the liver," Dr. L says. From the hospital down to the morgue, he might as well say. "It looks like the main tumor is attached to your liver, and it has spread to the pleura." I wish desperately for him to stop, but he keeps on giving blows.

"It will be a challenge in itself to get rid of, but the real challenge will be keeping it at bay." He pauses. "If there is anything we can do to help ..."

I knew it. "If." He said "if"! "If" means I'm going to die. Am I going to die? Is this what dying feels like? I look down at the spot where the wall meets the floor. I keep on staring at the same spot, trying to hold on to something that isn't there anymore. I walk out into the hall. Numbly shuffling a few meters, I then lean against a wall and let myself slide down till my butt touches the floor. On the floor, there's no danger of falling. My father comes out what seems hours later, but that's not possible. There are too many other unlucky ones to be told they are going to die. I don't dare look him in the eyes, scared of what I will see.

Our next stop is the radiology ward, where I'm injected with radioactive fluid so that they can do a bone scan. My father turns to leave the room. Well, that's great. If he can't even handle this, what the hell am I supposed to do? He comes back bleary-eyed, which he unsuccessfully tries to hide. I later find out that he went to call my mother and sister. The change in the eyes of my family will turn out to be the worst part of this whole nightmare: my father falling to his knees when he thinks I'm not watching; my mother crouching on the stairs, crying on the phone in the middle of the night; my sister unable to touch me without tears welling up in her eyes.

The injection requires two hours to take effect, which gives us just enough time to go home for an hour. I can't bear to spend another second in this place.

"This is not good, Dad," I say. "Not good at all."

"Sophie, they were just as negative with your mother. This year is going to be hell, but next year everything will be back to normal."

"That's bullshit, Dad. We both know this isn't breast cancer they're talking about!"

"That's just the way doctors are," he states firmly.

And that's just the way fathers are, I think.

As we turn onto our street, I make out my sister's silhouette waiting in front of the house. Saskia. I always call her Sis. We have the same dark eyebrows and full lips, but our personalities couldn't be more different. Sis is the consummate older sister: methodical, confident, responsible. Whereas I am the classic youngest child: stubborn, rebellious. The only thing we see eye to eye on is not getting along. After seven years of constant fighting, the rift between us just seems too big to fix.

But, bizarrely, Saskia is the one I most want to see. I sob into her open arms.

"Sis, I'm only twenty-one," I stammer. "I have cancer. I might die." She holds me close. I can feel her trembling. We go into the house, both crying. It's the first time in years that we've hugged. It feels good.

When we get inside I go up to my room and sit down in front of my mirror. I stare at my reflection, searching for something strange, something that isn't me, something that doesn't belong there. Something cancerous. All I see is a pale and frightened little girl. *Is that me? Am I a girl with cancer? Is this what a girl with cancer looks like?*

I think about my mother coming home on the tram. I'm sure she's found a spot in a corner, staring into the distance through the window. Maybe the tram is packed and she has to stand squashed between all those wet raincoats. Or has it stopped raining? I can't remember. I'm too busy crying, shedding more tears over this fucking cancer. *Why didn't she just take a taxi home, today of all days?* Maybe she needed time to process the news, or to pretend for a few more minutes that it was still just a normal day. First her cancer, and now my cancer. I wish I could be with her, support her, even though I can hardly keep myself upright.

I'm on the toilet when I hear her walking up the stairs toward me. She has this way of walking up and down the stairs: it will never go unnoticed. I quickly zip up my jeans and flush away my nervous pee. My jeans hang loosely around my butt—now I know I can thank the cancer for that. She comes bounding up the stairs and grabs my arms. Her eyes are moist but she isn't crying as she stares into my eyes. "We are going to get through this," she says over and over.

I just nod.

"Repeat after me, Sophie: We are going to get through this. We are going to get through this." She makes me say it countless times. I hold on to the words as tightly as I can. I don't stop repeating the mantra, even as we go back to the hospital for the bone scan. *Bone scan.* It sounds so ominous.

My grandmother has joined the brigade—she, my dad, and my sister are waiting downstairs in the hospital's depressing cafeteria while my mom, who was under the same machine not so long ago, takes me by the hand and leads the way. I have to take off anything metallic but am allowed to keep on my clothes. The room we're in is enormous, but the machine itself somehow seems even larger.

As I hand my mother my jewelry and bra, she presses her lucky chestnut into my hands. Keeping chestnuts is a family tradition, one that started with my grandmother, *oma*. Come autumn, we each pick up the most beautiful chestnut we can find and keep them in our pockets for good luck throughout the rest of the year. Anytime I slip my hand in my mother's pocket to keep it warm as we walk together, I know I'll find a chestnut. The one she's given me is the same one she carried through her own cancer treatment. She doesn't let go of me until she is convinced I have adopted her second mantra to chant during the scan: "It's not in my bones. It's not in my bones. It's not in my bones." If the cancer isn't in my bones, it means I have a chance. I repeat her words while stroking the chestnut so hard I'm afraid it might crack.

The scan takes about twenty minutes. During that time, everyone else has to leave the room because of the radiation. I enjoy the sudden peace and quiet and somehow end up falling asleep, which is as heavenly as waking up is difficult.

When it's over, my mother and I sit down in the row of chairs lining the hallway. I don't really know why; we won't even get the results until the following week. Maybe we both need to exhale.

The technician in charge of the scan comes outside. My mom looks up at him, her face as tense as an elastic wire. He holds his step and breaks the silence. "It looks good." I don't understand. Isn't that for the doctor to decide? I assume he means the pictures have turned out well. You know, like good positioning and no blurriness. Luckily, my mother is a bit more alert than I am. The tension must have been so visible on our faces that the technician decided to informally bring us the good news straightaway. He has to repeat himself three times before it sinks in. My mother jumps up and starts hugging him. I follow suit. Two cheeks, two women, two sets of lips. He hardly knows what to do with himself.

We run off in search of the rest of the family. My father is just turning down the hallway. I run toward him down the long, empty corridor, shouting: "Dad! Dad, it's not in my bones! My bones are clean, I'm going to get better!" I fling myself into his arms and he falls to his knees. Later he tells me that this is the moment he most vividly remembers from those horrible early days.

But this is hardly the end of the tests. The next day I'm scheduled for a bone marrow sample. Going back to that awful hospital is the last thing I want to do. My knees start to tremble the moment I walk in. I hate my new doctor and everything about him. He pulls out a long needle and what looks like a screwdriver and goes to work in the neighborhood of my hip. He warns me it will hurt, but by this point pain is my last concern. The fear has numbed me so much that I barely even notice as he drills into my bone.

Mom holds on to both my hands and looks me straight in the eye. I'm twenty-one; I'm supposed to be an adult, a grown-up who can take care of herself, but I'm scared shitless. I'm so afraid, I can't stop shivering. Afraid of doctors and their words, a language completely deprived of empathy and nice vocabulary. Afraid of cancer. And, most of all, afraid of what's still to come.

I'm left with a small hole in my side, which the nurse covers up with a big white bandage. "There we go, all done. You did really well." She's sweet, with a short, trendy haircut and flashy earrings. For a little longer than necessary we share glances. I recognize her. She treated my mother a few times during her chemo. How sweet life can be.

SATURDAY, JANUARY 29

I stare into the camera and stick up both of my middle fingers in defiance, telling my cancer to go fuck itself. It's Saturday and everything is different now. Different from yesterday, different from last week, different from last year. I didn't go to the market this morning or drink coffee on Westerstraat. On Monday, instead of going to class, I'll be checking into the hospital for my first week of chemotherapy treatment. For the next two months, I am expected each week for a dose of vincristine, etoposide, and ifosfamide and God knows what.

I'm at my good friend Jan's studio, with the Rolling Stones blaring through the speakers. I love Mick Jagger's raw voice and the rip of Keith Richards's guitar. I asked Jan to document me without cancer. Because after Monday, I'll be different: I'll be a cancer patient.

But today I've decided I don't have cancer. I'm smiling, pouting, making all sorts of faces for the camera; I'm free. It's the furthest I've been from tears since I got the news. This is the first time since last week that I'm not being comforted or trying to comfort someone else. In front of the lens, I feel myself growing bigger and stronger. I don't feel sad and weak. *I am going to get through this*. With every click of the shutter, I grow, I let loose completely. My eyes glisten with emotion. I'm still afraid, but here, in front of the camera, my fear changes into anger.

MONDAY, JANUARY 31

VITA BREVIS reads the stone gable on the building across the canal from our house. I've stared at those words from my bedroom window my entire life. It's the tallest and broadest building on the block, reaching up far above the other houses. It's hard to miss, but today those words speak to me in a way they've never spoken to me before. *Vita brevis:* Life is short.

I gather my things and walk outside, packed and ready to go to the hospital for my first week of chemo sessions. I've got so much stuff it looks like I'm going on vacation. My mother, sister, and I watch as my dad packs the car. From their faces I can tell that this is all just as frightening for them as it is for me. Frankly, they seem as sick as I do. The only thing that separates us is that the cancer is inside my body, and not in theirs. But this separation is not made before we get to the hospital, where there is one bed waiting, with my name on it.

When I arrive at my ward, C6, I am assigned to a shared room. Next to my bed there's an old woman crawling around on the floor by her bed, making strange screeching noises. She makes me question which ward I'm in. Oncology or psychiatric/neurology? The two other beds are taken by men old enough to be my grandfather. My heart sinks—I don't want to be surrounded by three old folks who already have one foot in the grave, even without having cancer. Looking at them, all I see is death. Teary-eyed, I plead with Dr. L, aka Dr. Prick, to be given a private room, just for my misery and me, but he doesn't budge. Luckily the nurse on duty, Bas, takes pity on me. He immediately starts running around switching bed assignments. If I'm in a room of my own, looking at my own white walls, maybe I can fool myself that I'm just passing through.

Bas doesn't look like a typical nurse. He has a shaved head and his arms are covered in tattoos. A thick silver necklace hangs around his neck. Not the type you would think to bring to your family's Christmas dinner. It turns out that I have let myself be fooled by appearances again: he's one big teddy bear. On the way to my new room we pass an office with nurses and a few doctors milling around inside. They look up and take note of the newcomer. We exchange hesitant smiles.

My new room is nothing to write home about, but it's all mine and I'm thankful. Bas doesn't waste any time and tells me in a single breath that I have my own bathroom and that I will lose all my hair after about three weeks.

"All my hair?"

"Yes."

"Even my eyebrows and eyelashes?" I ask.

"Those as well."

"And my pubic hair?"

"Yes, that, too."

"Great. A prepubescent pussy."

"Isn't that the fashion these days?"

"True."

I run my fingers through my hair and wonder what my head underneath looks like. My hair has never been red carpet material, but today I am more than happy with what I've got.

Chemotherapy is much less exciting than it sounds. I will be bedbound twenty-four hours a day. For eight of those hours I will be hooked up to an IV of chemo drugs. For the remaining sixteen I will be hooked up to an IV of water to flush out those drugs.

Thrilling.

Bas whistles as he hooks up some bags to the IV tube coming out of my arm. It looks innocuous enough—a bag of yellow stuff next to two bags of clear fluid. Bas fiddles around with the tube while another white coat makes notes on my file. I watch as the tube connected to my arm slowly fills with the yellow fluid. I carefully observe the yellow creeping closer and closer to my vein.

"Is this the chemo?"

"Yes."

I don't know if I want to take my arm away from this yellow gunk or if I want to leave it where it is and surrender. "Will it make me throw up?"

"It might," says Bas, "but not necessarily. Do you see this bag?" He points to one of the clear ones. "It's an antinausea drug."

The name of this miracle drug is dexamethasone. It has one unfortunate side effect, though: fluid retention. Within an hour I look and feel like a puffer fish from all the fluids I'm holding in. My cheeks are red and my face and arms are completely swollen. I don't throw up but it feels as if I have to, which is much worse than actually throwing up. Finally, my stomach can't take it, and a wave of bile comes out. I can smell my last meal: a tuna salad sandwich. *No more tuna salad for me. Ever.* I am nauseous for the rest of the day, but luckily I only vomit that one time.

My first bonus.

TUESDAY, FEBRUARY 1

My family turned my hospital room into a command center. My mom stays with me twenty-four hours a day so that we can sleep off this nightmare together. She spends each night on a cot next to my bed. Although I don't have much to do, sleeping in is not part of the package. Every morning at seven we are woken by the morning crew: nurses, needles, and a shrill lady pushing a coffee cart. The cancer brings me back to being a little girl who desperately needs her mom. Every time I have to go to the toilet she detaches my IV pump from its socket, and when I feel too sick to get up she brushes my teeth with one hand and holds a spit bowl under my chin with the other. She helps the nurses to look after me, and when I sleep she watches over me.

My father takes care of the business side of things, doing background checks on my doctor with all his medical friends and researching my disease. He has lunches and dinners in private clubs and calls it work, and as far as I know that's what he does between nine A.M. and nine P.M. He's been talking to everyone in the hospital, and now he's heard about the Mayo Clinic in America and has turned it into his new project. In the past few days he has developed more of a relationship with my doctor than I have. While I look the other way, my father chases Dr. L to offer his latest advice on my treatment. I myself am not so keen on contact with Dr. L. To me, he is just as nasty as my disease.

I'm happy to leave the research to my father. When I first got my diagnosis I tried to do the research thing, but I failed miserably at it. When I typed "rhabdomyosarcoma" into the Internet search bar it generated 846,000 hits. *So much for a rare cancer.* The statistics weren't much better. I slammed shut the lid of my laptop. It felt as if each one of those hits killed one of my dreams.

So far the cancer has brought one good thing: I have my sister back. Our fights are a thing of the past. The looks we exchange are different. The hostility is gone. Love has taken its place. It's maybe strange to say, lying in a hospital bed at all, but every time she walks in I feel really happy.

Sis has her role too. She keeps everything going at home, which is much more than feeding our blind, demented cat and taking out the trash. She makes sure my father eats proper meals and that Mom is surprised with phone calls, sandwiches, and glossy magazines. Where she finds the time to do all that, finish writing her thesis, and visit me, I have no idea, but she shows up at the hospital every day armed with fresh pasta, organic soup, body lotion, and a beaming smile.

Me, I have only one job: to get sick and then get better. That's what chemo does to your body. So that's what I do. The only thing on my to-do list is survival. I lie in bed, determined to leave this mess behind me. Nothing moves me, not even the pain I feel when they insert the IV or when I'm throwing up into a bucket between my mother's hands. I don't know if I feel depressed or if this is what depression is like. I do know that I've never felt so empty in my entire life.

WEDNESDAY, FEBRUARY 2

"Look at the state of her! It's completely unacceptable. If you don't do something about it immediately, I'm going to take the poor thing out of here myself."

From inside my room I can hear my friends Jan and Jochem, scolding Dr. L in the hallway. Jan, a well-known TV host and enfant terrible of the Netherlands, can get away with basically anything—whether he's hosting his TV talk show or hounding my doctor. I can hear Dr. L speak uncomfortably to Jan, and it makes me smile.

My head has expanded from a puffer fish to the size of a football the color of a tomato, and my arms do not even remotely resemble their old shapes. That I am about three kilos heavier than yesterday does not escape Jan's and Jochem's attention.

"Hey, cutie! You're positively glowing today. That shade of crimson is very becoming on you." Jan produces a carton of fresh blueberry juice from his bag. "For the antioxis or something."

Jochem presents me with two more bottles of dark red fluid. The label reads ELDERBERRY. "I asked for the one with the most vitamins," he says quietly. "The lady behind the counter said this is really good for you." He bends over and kisses me on the cheek.

Besides my family, there's only a handful of people I'm happy to have around me these days. There's my best friend

Annabel and then there's Jan, Jochem, and Rob, number three of the gang. We've all met in the café where I work on Sundays. Well, used to.

The boys are a great gift as they are always available (being retired, freelance, and jobless) and make me laugh the whole time, but it is Annabel who visits me nearly every day. We have known each other since we were learning to read and write in kindergarten. Since then not a day has gone by that we don't know what the other is doing, and with whom.

As we are very different characters but both Geminis, Annabel explains that there are two kinds of Geminis: those with more characteristics of a Taurus and those with more of the Cancer sign. According to her, she's more Taurus and I'm more Cancer. Well, we've just about proven that bit. I never really pay attention, but I'm sure she has an astrological explanation for why she went on to study marketing at university while I opted for political science. Annabel is not just my partner in crime but also my fashion guru; somehow between the Chanel tops and vintage bags we find time to discuss solar energy, inflation, and genocide in the developing world.

We discovered the world together. As small girls, as teenagers, and now as supposedly adults. We've eaten snails in the Dordogne and sweets in the harbor of Copenhagen. We've stood openmouthed beneath Josephine Baker's chandelier in her French château filled with bats. We've swum, screeching, through seaweed in Denmark and bought our first pair of velvet lady shoes in a boutique in London.

We have only ever been apart twice. First when I left for the Himalayas and later when Annabel went to do an internship in New York, where she worked in a small fashion house specializing in bridal couture. She'd just returned when cancer entered our lives, though looking back we could both see the signs that something had been wrong. I went to visit her in December, to celebrate Christmas and New Year's together. She'd be three blocks and two Starbucks ahead of me while I was still panting my way up the city's endless subway steps. And it definitely wasn't like me to be partied out by one A.M. on New Year's Eve when there was a cute New Yorker standing in front of me. Luckily I wasn't too tired to stow away his business card in a safe place. The card led to Sunday morning at MoMA, which turned into Sunday afternoon at Pastis, which ended up in a romantic dinner with plenty of red wine, which ended up in bed. The next day I woke up coughing and trembling on the Lower East Side. I was covered in sweat and felt sick. I also felt unattractive, wet and sweaty and all. I left his room as silently as I could. It was still dark out when I closed the door behind me.

This is the second time the boys have come to visit me. Last time Jan brought me a lollipop in the shape of a heart; Jochem brought a bunch of flowers. And, of course, Jan always comes with a pile of tabloids and magazines. They make a fuss when the nurses come in bearing needles, telling them to keep their hands off me.

Today it's Nurse Bas who comes in to reinsert my IV. As soon as he brings out the needle, Jan's and Jochem's expressions change. They turn silent and carefully step aside. For once, neither of them makes a joke. I'm not one of the guys anymore; I'm a sick puffer fish hooked up to an IV.

SATURDAY, FEBRUARY 5

There is a knock at the door. It's the not-so-charming doctor from the pulmonary department who told me I have cancer. Poor guy, it's not his fault he just happened to be taking over for my beloved Dr. K on that particular day. I jump when his head suddenly appears from behind the curtain that closes off my bed from the rest of the hospital (and everything walking, throwing up, and screeching around inside it). He wants to know how I'm doing. *Besides the nausea and bloated head from all the drugs being pumped into me?* I tell him I'm fine.

Yes, I tell everyone who asks that I'm fine. Don't ask me why.

He leaves and the tall figure of Dr. L appears, with a swarm of students following him. Without any warning they simply walk in, take up position, and start staring.

Surrounded around my bed, twelve eyes bore into me.

I hate it when he brings them along. It's embarrassing and awkward to be looked at like a science experiment, not giving me a moment to comb my hair or something. But I guess that should be the least of my worries now.

"Good morning, we've come to take a look at you," says Dr. L.

Duh, I can see that. I look past the collection of strange doctors from the oncology and hematology departments, scanning for Dr. McDreamy, who came to visit me every day and ask after Anna Karenina. Who had been kind enough to help me pull down my camisole over my shaking back the day he'd drained the fluid, when it wasn't clear yet that an entire family of tumors had attached itself to my lung. (Correction: to the fleece surrounding my lung, also called pleural space.) But Dr. K is not among them.

There is something different about Dr. L today: he's smiling. It's the first time I've ever seen him do that.

"I have two pieces of good news. One: we have the definitive lab results back, and your bones are indeed clean. Two: we have taken another look at your photos and have come to the conclusion that the cancer is only in the pleura. That means the tumors are limited to the thorax and have not yet penetrated the right abdomen. The stinging you feel around your liver is just a shooting pain. Which means there is the probability of dissemination, but it is not organ-to-organ, and although I can't guarantee anything since your illness is quite rare and the lab still isn't sure of the exact diagnosis, this could make the prognosis better."

Silence. I don't really understand what he has just said. Bones, organ-to-organ dissemination, thorax? But Mom makes a high-pitched noise and starts to sob. That's quite rare for her: she's not a crier. Slowly I realize that she's crying tears of joy. *This is good news. Really good news!* Dr. L is telling me my liver is clean—and by now I know that cancer in the liver usually means picking out a spot at the cemetery.

I can't help but smile. My mom squeezes my hand.

"It's still going to be a long treatment," Dr. L continues. "We're going to schedule you for fifty-four weeks of chemo. For now you'll come in every week for treatment. Later on we'll reduce it to every three weeks. Once this IV drip is done, you can go home for the weekend. I'll see you on Monday."

When he leaves, Mom is still sobbing.

THURSDAY, FEBRUARY 17

I look in the mirror at the lady standing behind me. Strange hands pick through what's left of my hair. Clumps fall to my feet. She doesn't look like the kind of lady I would take fashion advice from, but today I haven't been given a choice. This time of my life seems to be all about surrender.

Wig shopping isn't new to me, but I never thought I would be wig shopping for myself. Last year my mother went through the same hell during her breast cancer. I accompanied her to two shops, and I didn't bring any good memories back of those visits. They were weird places with saleswomen trying to make us feel we were out shopping for something nice. At the time my mother still wore her hair piled on top of her head. Now it's short and messy.

She underwent two operations to cut out as much of the cancer as possible, followed by five weeks of radiation, and then chemotherapy at the same hospital where I am now a patient. It was a scary time for all of us. The doctors' words became increasingly more frightening, from surgery to radiation to chemo. The last stage was the worst. Chemo and death seem so close together.

We did leave with a wig for my mother, but it all felt very mechanical. There was none of the joy or relief that comes with finding something that makes you prettier, or just what you have been looking for. A woman in despair, deprived of her hair and her femininity. A saleswoman holding a soft hazelnut-brown wig that came closest to the hairdo my mother had said good-bye to. Then the sound of a bank card being swiped and a white plastic bag on the counter. My mother rarely wore it, preferring to wrap her head in a scarf. I never told her this, but to me the wig always looked unnatural.

This morning there was hair on *my* pillow when I woke up. Clumps of hair in my hairbrush. Despair in the sink. Nurse Bas was right. Three weeks to the day. It's the strangest thing: yesterday my hair was still glued to my scalp. I even believed for a minute that maybe chemo wouldn't affect me the way it affects others.

While the saleswoman leaves to search for wigs that would suit me, I gently run my fingers through my hair, a new bunch of strands coming out with every touch. I look at a brush lying on the table. It's evil. The clumps, the brush, the mirror.

The wig shop is situated in the central lobby of the hospital. That's called practicality. *This way the oncology patients can stop by straight after being unhooked from the IV.* Sitting beside me are my mother, sister, and Annabel. We're all quiet and uncomfortable, until Annabel breaks the tension by trying on one of the wigs. It looks ridiculous. We burst out laughing.

I see the saleswoman taking a wig out of its box. *Be positive, Sophie!* I fail. "I'm losing tons every day," I say as she combs my hair. She looks at me in the mirror. I've brought pictures with me of how I like to wear my hair. They are the ones Jan took three weeks ago, when I still had a full head of it. I look less and less like that girl from the pictures now that my hair cells are losing the fight against the chemo. The pictures are lying on the table, next to a brochure for wigs and a sample of yellow-blonde hair that has just appeared. *Maybe something like this? Not even close.* All these hairdos make me look like a drag queen, and when she presents me with a bunch of long dark hair, all I can think of is that guitar player in Guns N' Roses. It might work for MTV, but not on my head.

Disastrous.

I look at my sister, with her dark hair twisted up in a bun. She looks beautiful. She wears her hair up and pushed back, slightly messy. I look at Annabel's thick black hair, again at my sister's shiny locks, then at my mother's short do and back to the few pathetic wisps left on my head. The past three weeks whiz through my mind, but I still can't quite grasp how I got here.

I want to escape, to hide behind the safe walls of my home. Not just from this disease, but also from the reactions of those around me that confirm everything I want to forget. Neighbors with pity in their eyes. The man in the grocery store sneaking an extra bunch of vitamins into my shopping basket. Friends hugging me tight. Family crying along with me. I look into the mirror with glistening eyes and let the lady fiddle around with my hair. Of my full lips, only a sad stripe remains, running straight across my face. The more she pulls at my hair, the thinner the stripe and the more lost I feel.

In the end, nothing looks right and I choose a prissy head of hair that comes closest to the way I used to look but that somehow doesn't look like me at all. It's ugly and it itches like crazy.

The woman is talking to me encouragingly.

"It will take a little while for it to feel like 'you.' A wig never feels right on the first day, but play around with it, try it out, and within two weeks it will be totally you." She's been in this business for twenty years and claims she's one of the few who works with the hip, young wigs from Japan. "That's where all the fun, fresh looks come from. Perfect for young girls like you."

"This is a hip, young wig from Japan?" *It's practically a beehive! Poufy and outdated.* This isn't me. This is some housewives haircut who lost all interest in life. In an attempt to find something that looks the most like me, I end up with something that doesn't look like me at all. How did that happen?

I turn around to my mother and see that she, too, is close to tears.

In the elevator I look for myself in the mirror. A strange woman looks back at me.

FRIDAY, FEBRUARY 18

"You look exactly like that Vermeer girl, the one with the pearl earring."

It's a big improvement over what springs to my mind whenever I see my new reflection in the mirror. After a long session experimenting with Annabel's headbands and the hair spray in a weird white canister that came with the wig, I come down to the kitchen around midday. My mother and her friend Maud are having coffee. I smile, kiss Maud's cheek, and fill the kettle.

"I swear, the spitting image," I can hear her continue. It's a sweet thing to say, but that's all it is. Mom smiles at her friend. I scratch my head aggressively, hopelessly trying to combat the eternal itching. I need to get rid of the last few hairs; they itch like crazy and make my head look even sicker.

I disappear back upstairs to the mirror. In front of me on the chest of drawers lies a large agenda, one of those professional day planners. It is dedicated to the fifty-four weeks of chemo and radiation which sums up my life for the next fifty-three weeks. The first week is triumphantly crossed out.

In the ninth week I will have my first evaluation. I'll be scanned to see if all the throwing up has been good for anything at all. I'm scared to death. That the next scan could also mean my life will take a turn for the better is something I won't allow myself to consider. It will only make the blow harder to bear when it comes. I try to contemplate the worst-case scenario: the tumors growing, the cancer incurable, me at the end of the road. I pick up our old cat, Saartje, and hold her close while I wonder who will outlive whom. For the first time in my life, I become aware of my own mortality, of being human, a part of a cycle much bigger than myself, where there's no room or need for individuality.

Today is the first day I reach for the wig—after putting on my mascara. For the moment I still have eyebrows and eyelashes. When will they go? I'm shuffling through the house in my mother's slippers and a soft, fluffy white dressing gown, which I got from the greatest boyfriend in the world. Unfortunately he's not mine but my sister's. Even so, I get some of the perks. The theme of my life these days is receiving, receiving, and even more receiving. Flowers, gifts, hugs. And I need it all—I soak it in like a sponge, not having anything left to give back in return.

I have to admit, I wouldn't mind having a boyfriend of my own these days telling me I'm still pretty, showing me that I'm still a girl worthy of snuggling up to. It would make the nights a lot less lonely. But at least I have my sister back. Sometimes she leaves her beau alone and cuddles up next to me. I like listening to her when she talks about her daily life, but hearing her talk about her future hurts. I don't have any future to talk about. I want her to be happy, but it's difficult, very difficult when you don't have something to be happy about yourself.

I feel heavy and numb, even though my body seems to be disappearing before my eyes. The scales show another pound gone. Same as every day this week. I have discovered the perfect diet: fear, stress, and tumor sweat. The night sweats started a few months ago, another one of my inexplicable symptoms before the diagnosis, but they were never as intense as they are now. I wake up a few times a night bathed in sweat. Concave belly, heaving rib cage. Everything soaking wet, either from sweat or tears. "Tumor fever," they call it. For me it starts every night at nine. This morning, at four A.M., I peeled off another drenched T-shirt reeking of tumor sweat. There are four others beside my bed, two dirty and two clean. My mother unfolded a fresh T-shirt and helped me pull it on. My body leads a life of its own, responding to something I can't see that has taken control. It's times like these that my disease is closer than ever.

I've been sleeping in my parents' bedroom. Not something to brag about at age twenty-one, but it's just the way it is. I'm back to being the little girl I once was.

"I'm so scared," I whispered into my pillow last night.

My dad wrapped his arms around me. "Sophie, you mean everything to me."

I released myself into his big embrace. My body was damp to the touch. After a while my mother joined us.

"What if I die?" I held them tightly and looked over my father's shoulders through a slit in the curtains. The slit was just wide enough to see the night. A bare tree, a piece of the not so friendly gable stone of the house on the opposite side of the canal, a sliver of moonlight, a dark backdrop.

"You are not going to die." My mother's voice.

"But what if I do? What if my tumors don't go away? I am so afraid of the scan." My whole body felt as if it were weeping.

"So are we, Sophie, so are we." My father looked at me helplessly. I felt relieved that he let me speak about my greatest fear and didn't try to brush it away. It's exhausting to put on a brave face when behind it there is only fear. Still I keep on doing so.

* * *

The few hairs still clinging to my scalp itch like crazy and look ridiculous. I decided not to wait any longer and called up Sis to see if she can help me out with the task. She's at the door half an hour later with an electric razor. Maud gets up and leaves us alone.

"This is supposed to be a really good one, I just picked it up from a friend who works as a hairdresser," my sister says.

She and my mother hold up a mirror while I switch on the razor. We are sitting at the kitchen table, three pairs of eyes fixed on my hands steering the machine carefully but determinedly over my scalp. Although there's not that much left to shave, I feel a burst of strength running through me: shaving myself into a skinhead before the cancer can do.

In a few minutes' time it's done. While shaving, I managed to look only at my hair and not at my face. But now that it's finished I am as bald as a bowling ball. *I look revolting*. I tell myself that G.I. Jane did the same thing and she was still a hot chick, but it doesn't make me feel any better. For the next few weeks I avoid every mirror. I hate my new head, with or without wig.

MONDAY, MARCH 14

Six weeks have passed since my first admission to C6. Today I'm back in the hospital to be admitted for the second time. I have to be admitted twice in a nine-week cycle, in the first and seventh weeks. During the in-between weeks, I go in for my shots and injections at the day-patient ward, which takes only a few hours. This routine changes again after the first block—the first nine weeks; my schedule is demanding and I barely understand it. Doctors like to make things complicated, it seems.

When I'm not doing chemo, I spend most of my time resting or going back to the hospital to get my blood checked. In short, my life as a patient is almost as busy as it was as a full-time student, running between classes, dates, and part-time jobs. So busy that I'm starting to enjoy random things like brushing my teeth in my own bathroom at home, walking out for grocery shopping, getting dressed, watching TV. It's all quite a feast compared to lying in C6 with a tube stuck in me.

Today is Sis's birthday—she's twenty-five. A quarter century already. Despite everything, I've always known that I love her, but knowing and feeling are two different things. Knowing is two-dimensional. Feeling is tangible. I now carry that feeling with me the way I carry mam's chestnut with me. I enjoy it strongest when she's caressing my back as I fall asleep, but also when she's just sitting next to me at the kitchen table, absorbed in her studies.

We've gone through all the sisterhood stages: best friends, best foes, and now back to best friends. She's always been very caring, the person who silently moves around the house to make sure everybody's okay. When our mother turns moody, she silently goes and does what needs to be done, while I am too occupied with being moody because of my mothers' moodiness.

The other morning Sis she came up with a cup of tea. She sat with me till I woke up. She would do this sometimes when we were still kids. I had forgotten about these cups of tea.

Dr. L stops by to see how I'm coping with the side effects of the chemotherapy and to check the color of my cheeks. He mumbles something, looks uncomfortable, and gets down to business as soon as he possibly can.

"Are you noticing any tingling in your fingertips and toes?" he asks. "We need to keep a close eye on the side effects of the vincristine because you're getting plenty of it."

I shake my head. No tingling, but I have been feeling stabbing pains everywhere since the chemo started. As if fighting my disease had truly woken it up and sent it raging throughout my body. I start to wonder why we aren't called "chemo patients" instead of "cancer patients." It's hard to feel the difference between the stabs from the chemo and those from the cancer. Sometimes I get an overwhelming premonition that the cancer has spread through my entire body, but one of Dr. L's assistants has done a good job of convincing me that this is almost impossible—a shame Dr. L himself doesn't possess that gift.

"Your HB, your red blood cell count, is a little low"—doctor-speak for "You look washed out"—"so at the end of this week I'll give you a blood transfusion. There is always a small risk attached to transfusions"—a risk of like one in a million, that is—"but I prefer them over EPO."

"EPO?"

"A hormonal injection to stimulate the production of red blood cells in your bone marrow. It could also stimulate the growth of your tumors."

"Oh. Like Lance?"

"Something like that. And how are the night sweats?"

Dr. L sure knows how to keep a conversation going. The tumor sweat has been pouring from my body for the past few weeks and has my parents in its hypnotic grip. On the worst nights my bed is remade three times and my T-shirts changed up to five times. I keep getting weaker and losing more weight.

"It's getting better, but last two nights were pretty wet."

"That's not a good sign." My mention of "getting better" goes unnoticed. "We'll have to keep an eye on it."

Nearly two months have gone by, but as far as I'm concerned, Dr. L is still the nasty man who turned my whole life upside down. As if he's the one to blame for the tumors in my body. He's the one who gave them a name, after all. His nametag says DR. L, but the nurses call him by his first name. So do I. Calling him "Prick" to his face might not be the best idea. He comes by virtually every day, to see how his cancer-patient vegetable garden is doing. His bedside manner varies between rude, stiff, and socially awkward. Toward his patients, that is: I often hear him laughing and joking with his colleagues. He's clearly one of those docs who prefers to hide behind their medical jargon, without ever offering his patients a glimmer of hope. He wants nothing to do with the psyche or positive thinking; after all, you can't measure that.

But he is also my doctor, my hope, and my healer. My medical magician. I'm not talking a wand and disappearing bunny rabbits, though. No, he is pure medical science; honesty and persistence to help all his patients get rid of their cancer nightmares. When it comes to being my savior, nobody else comes close. Not even Dr. K.

This is the first week I'm shuffling around the hospital with my bald head. I can't decide which is uglier: Sophie with a beehive or Sophie as a skinhead. So I've wound a scarf around my head, and you wouldn't be able to tell me apart from the cleaning lady who comes in each day with her bucket of chlorine and a mop. Nurse Bas calls me "Baldy" now. When he says it, it makes me laugh. I started calling him Nurse Betty—he's the only male nurse on this ward and I feel that he deserves some special recognition. At eight o'clock he wakes me up with "Morning, Baldy"—like I'm the only one on this floor—and helps me pull on a clean top. It can be quite a challenge with all these tubes coming out of my wrists. After that he gives me a pat on the head and sits down for a chat as he changes the bandage around my wrist meant to keep all that tubing in place.

"Making a lovely mess again, I see."

"You try moving around with all these tubes sticking out of you!"

I am given two bags of blood to get my blood count back up and to replace sluggish me with active me. It's a strange concept to be using someone else's blood as a sort of drug to make me feel better. Maybe that's the reason I feel so different these days—why I no longer like sweet pastries or licorice. And why I suddenly love writing. It's all part of the changes brought on by the cancer—Before, I didn't like writing at all. I even paid Sis to write my school reports. This week I checked into the hospital with a laptop under my arm. Not for surfing the Web, but for surfing my thoughts. But now at night, lying wide-awake in bed, I get out of bed to grab a pen and a piece of paper with the urge to write some thoughts down. When morning comes, I have pages full of thoughts. Ever since, I can't stop. I write down everything that happens to me, clinging on to the words that come as if I'm clinging on to life.

Around ten thirty in the morning I take my shower. I take extra long to lather myself up with body wash, body lotion, and all my other tonics, just to kill time. Then I get dressed. Everything I put on goes up from my feet and then my hips, or else my IV gets in the way. I'm still as vain as ever; I brought all my prettiest camisoles with me in case Dr. K or another sexy doctor comes to visit. I'm not likely to meet anyone else in this prison. Every other day I have to leave the ward for tests elsewhere in the hospital. When that happens, I feel the attention I'm drawing: the cancer patient I don't want to be, shuffling along clumsily with my IV pushed out in front of me, the bags of chemo swaying back and forth. As soon as the tests are over, I retreat to my hospital bed and try to forget where I am. Try to forget I will wake up in the morning to discover all over again that there is not one hair growing on my head.

"Hi, sweetie, how are you feeling?"

I turn toward the familiar sound and see a big purple orchid enter my room, followed by Annabel.

"Honeybun!" I call out happily. "Is my wig on straight?"

Annabel looks me up and down and smiles. She pulls into place my beehive that I have come to name Stella because of her elderly looks.

"Do you ever think about what it would be like if I were gone?" I ask.

"Well, aren't you a little ray of sunshine today?" She sits down on the chair next to my bed and takes out her manicure set.

"I want to know what that thought means to you." Annabel is an expert at keeping her pain covered up, even for me.

"Yes. I think about it." She looks at me. "I might look tough, but I lie crying in Bart's arms every single night." (Bart is her boyfriend.) "But as long as there is hope I refuse to think the worst."

"Oh." That's Annabel. She just takes on and refuses life the way it suits her. A feeling of sympathy creeps up on me, but frankly I love hearing her say those words. The more she cries, the more she loves me. "We've always been together," I say.

"And we always will be."

Without Annabel I wouldn't know what it feels like to have a true friend, the kind who lies in her bed in Amsterdam and knows I'm feeling lonely in India. The kind of friend who is only a glance away from knowing what is really going on in my head. The kind who knew before my diagnosis that something was really wrong. The kind who braves a rush-hour tram with huge purple orchids to make my depressing white room feel a little bit more like home.

"Two more weeks. Scary, huh?"

"Until the scan?"

"Yes."

"Well, then there's no reason to ask ourselves silly questions today, is there?" She bends over and continues her manicure.

THURSDAY, MARCH 24

The bartenders at my local hangout Café Finch gave me a box set of *Sex and the City* as a present. In the latest episodes, Samantha has been wearing a different wig every night, each one more fabulous than the last. My theory is simple: if she can look fabulous and have cancer, I can too. Mostly, I just want to look and feel like a girl again rather than someone I don't want to be.

I head with Annabel to a theater-supply store on the other side of town. The place is literally filled with wigs from the floor to the ceiling. Annabel inspects them all intently, while a salesperson stands behind me tugging at Stella. It reminds me of when we were little girls at the grocery store and would stare wide-eyed at the raspberries, blueberries, and blackberries before mixing them up.

This is the first time Annabel will see my bald head. I'm worried that it will scare her. I swallow nervously, not daring to take off my wig. She must have noticed, as she gives me a smile and nods. I take it as an encouragement. If I can't be naked around her, with whom can I? When the wig comes off she looks at me intensely and then strokes my pink scalp a few times. "Nice and soft," she says. I choke back my tears.

The salesperson plunks a number of different wigs on my head, and then suddenly there she is: Daisy. All three of us see it straightaway; Daisy is a keeper. With long blonde curls falling over my shoulders, I look at the strange girl in the mirror. It feels amazing to run my fingers through the kind of thick long curls I've only ever dreamed of. My face is completely different; suddenly I'm mischievous and playful instead of old and stiff. I feel like a whole other person wearing Daisy. Someone concerned with summer dresses and Glastonbury rather than chemo and other life and death matters.

Annabel ties a pink scarf around my new do and then continues studying the rest of the wigs on display. She returns with a short and spicy red number. She looks even better on me. The red locks bring my pale cheeks to life. And the edgy cut brings out my boldness. On the spot, we decide to call her "Sue." I don't know why I find the name fitting; it just comes to me. Maybe because it's so short: Sue. Strong and decisive.

I leave the store with two new wigs, two new characters. Which suits Annabel's theory about Geminis all the better: apparently my type can't seem to decide.

Before long, I come home with Blondie, a short and sexy blonde bob. She's my only wig so far made out of real hair. That doesn't only make her my most favorite but also my most expensive: 800 euros. *Ridiculous*. But when I wear her and stroke my hands through my hair, it's as if I'm touching my own hair after using loads of conditioner. Again, she makes me feel different. Daisy is very much a Barbie, and Sue is headstrong, but Blondie makes me feel like an independent woman, even if the opposite is true.

I call each of my wigs by a different name because each brings out a different character, a different personality. A different woman. Looking different makes me act different and attract different responses. I am no longer Sophie but Stella, Daisy, Sue, or Blondie. Blonde is the main theme of my collection. I guess that means blondes do have more fun.

The test was easily done. Few men look up to Sue; many look up to Daisy and Blondie. They get more attention and more free drinks.

SUNDAY, MARCH 27

Outside it's still winter. The clock shows six thirty P.M.; when I look out of the window it is already dark. After a long week spent attached to the IV at the hospital, I'm snuggled up on the couch at home, knees jammed between my arms in an "I don't feel like taking a shower because I'll be going back to bed soon anyway" mind-set.

Computer on my lap, wearing my robe, and with freshly polished bright red toenails, I'm half watching *Bridget Jones's Diary* on TV and half typing. Pretty typical for any twenty-one-year-old girl. This kind of entertainment is the best distraction from what is continuously playing through my mind: the scan, only four days away. I get up and pull Daisy off my head. I look around for Sue and my right hand strokes my scalp. It may look awful, but it feels strangely nice and soft. I catch a glimpse of my reflection in the mirror. Luckily, my cheeks have returned to their regular proportions, the puffer fish temporarily deflated. I try to see the pretty girl I once was, but I can't. I try to see myself as myself, but I can't do that either. I quickly put on Sue and snuggle back on the couch.

A wig turns out to be so much more than a bunch of hair. Each one does something to me. It goes further, much further than the way I look: they affect my sense of self.

It's a complete transformation when I put Daisy on my head. Long curls cascade down my back. My Italian sandals become sexy stilettos, my jeans a hip-hugging skirt, and my humble cleavage becomes a real showstopper. That's why I love her. Daisy makes her best entrance when she's fashionably late and her curls are running wild. Everyone wants to know who's hiding behind those fairy-blonde ringlets.

As Daisy I like to attract all the attention: tossing my curls from side to side, laughing giddily at every joke, drinking milk shakes instead of tomato juice, and glossing my lips to the max. I prefer watching *Sex and the City* to reading Virgil, and my toenails absolutely must be red. I dream of romantic getaways with Dr. K—although that fantasy exists no matter which wig I'm wearing.

As Sue I have something most women don't: wild red locks. Making an impression is easy; I don't have to laugh at silly jokes or toss around my mane.

My first wig, Stella, makes me understand what I'm not. Or maybe I should say what I don't want to be. I don't really know the difference anymore at this point. Her hair is always the same, it never moves. It makes her come across quite rigid, there's not one hair that sticks out. I prefer them messy.

And Blondie makes me feel invisible—in a good way. It's not a haircut that stands out. She's perfect for the days when I don't want to be the center of attention. If I want to flirt or be noticed in a different way, I wear Daisy or Sue.

All four ladies have something in common. In all four there is a little bit of me. A Sophie who grows by stealing a little inspiration from them all. And a Sophie who can see the changes in herself by observing how these ladies tackle life. Together Daisy, Blondie, Sue, and Stella are forming a new me.

THURSDAY, MARCH 31

Breathe in and out deeply, but most important, lie very still. I have to take off all my jewelry, just like the first time, as well as my bra, but I get to keep my wig and sweater on because it's cold. I put on Sue this morning. She makes me feel undefeatable. I thought it might help (to change the course of things). I'm lying on a narrow examination table that is slowly sliding into a tunnel as long as my upper body. The machine overlooks my thorax and abdomen, chest and stomach.

I think about the past two months. They feel like a lifetime. Today marks such an enormous distance from my life before the cancer. I don't even remember how it feels to be a student chasing internship opportunities during the day and guys in the cafés at night. I don't even remember what my dreams looked like. So much has changed. My future is now a big blank. It's weird living with no tomorrow, when I've spent the past twenty years thinking that's all there is. Maybe that's why the past two months have felt so long. Now, today is all I have.

I swallow, quietly, so as not to interfere with the CT scan. It doesn't take long, maybe ten minutes. But I'm in there for more than half an hour because the radiologists can't get the IV into me to administer the contrast fluid that has to be pumped through my body first. They tell me I have tricky veins, that they are too thin, too deep, too hidden. I roll my eyes. That's what I hear them saying to everybody on the ward. Let them puncture holes in one another before they send me home with five new bruises.

Dr. L says he'll try to call me before the weekend to give me the news so I don't have to spend days waiting. I'm not sure whether I'm happy about it. I would rather have a weekend of hope than find out I have one weekend less to live.

When Sue and I get home my mother is as tense as an electric wire. All her muscles seem to have contracted, making her look like a statue. I think it's her way of keeping out the demons. It's strange how fear can make people look ice cold on the outside while they are actually boiling hot with love on the inside.

Suddenly the phone rings. I stopped answering it a few months ago—all the well-meaning chitchat is just too much for me—but I'm standing right next to it, and my arm instinctively picks it up. It's Dr. L. My entire body breaks out in a cold sweat and sends my heart racing. The world shrinks to the corner of the kitchen where I'm standing. Everything around me goes silent, only to silence: the conversation between my mother and the neighbor who came by a few minutes ago with fresh flowers, but also the sounds from the street outside. Only my breathing and the sound of Dr. L's voice remain.

"Well, Sophie, I've taken a look at the photos straightaway. The official report will follow, but ..." Then there is a long and complicated story that I can't follow. He seems to have forgotten that I'm the unwilling patient and don't share his scientific passion. He pauses.

"Is it good?" I ask tensely.

"Yes, Sophie, it's good."

A long, deep sigh. "Are you satisfied?"

"Yes, Sophie, I'm satisfied, but we're not out of the woods yet. There's a long road ahead of us."

Screaming erupts in our kitchen. I put my hand on my head, stroking Sue, thanking her in silence.

SATURDAY, APRIL 2

Today was actually a really nice day. It passed by without scary thoughts, and I just *enjoyed* being home. I don't recall being home ever being such a treat.

It was just Mom and me at the house. My dad was unwinding in a rowing tournament for veterans, and my sis had left for a romantic weekend with her still perfect boyfriend.

Mom walks up and down the stairs, cleaning, rearranging, cooking. She is always on the move. Someone must have told her when she was little that sitting still and leaning back is something that we do at night in bed, and if we are lucky at the very end of the day when everything that could be done is done.

But my being ill affected the household. She seems much more relaxed now. Although I assume she runs even faster up and down the stairs the weeks I'm at the hospital.

I'm sitting on one sofa watching a movie while the rain is attacking the high windows that overlook the canal. Mom sits on the other sofa, not fighting the stairs anymore, and sorting out her collection of little soldiers. Mom has all sorts of collections of antiques. When Sis and I were still small she had her own antique shop two streets up. Almost everything in our house has been found in antique shops or markets. Before Mom professionalized her hobby, she flew around the whole world as an air hostess for KLM in a smart blue suit. She left home quite early, eager to see the world and eager to close a certain door behind her, the one of her parents arguing too often. In those years, being an air hostess came with many advantages: luxury hotels, enough days to visit and enjoy the destinations, and serving her favorite actor, Robert Redford, another glass of champagne.

It's where she met Maud, one of her friends I like most. Maud once told me that she was intrigued by my mother, who wore red lipstick and permed her hair even though KLM rules restricted it. It's only when I see them together and they start laughing or digging up memories that I realize my mom has been a girl too.

SUNDAY, APRIL 3

It's busy today on the Noordermarkt. Shoppers, vendors, bread, mushrooms, flowers, crowded terraces, apple pie. Sun and blue skies galore. I arrive outside Café Winkel just before one o'clock. Today I'm Daisy, light and careless. I feel as energetic as a squeezed lemon, but Daisy is full of laughter and life. That's what I call an easy pick. Wearing a pair of large black sunglasses, a black hairband, and a mane of long blonde curls, I scan the terrace for a boy I'm meeting named Jurriaan. Like me, he was diagnosed with cancer when he was twenty-one. Today he's twenty-six and full of energy.

Beneath one of the umbrellas on the terrace, a young man sits reading the newspaper. I take off my sunglasses.

"Are you Jurriaan?"

The young man looks up. "No."

"Oh, I'm sorry." I walk on and take a seat farther up the terrace.

"Sophie?" I look up into a set of dark eyes. "Hi, I'm Jurriaan. Have we met before? You look familiar." That's nice to hear after the big transformation.

He takes a seat next to me. Three kisses on two cheeks. Jurriaan is wearing a blue T-shirt, not too baggy. The perfect cut to show off a great body. A pair of Nikes on his feet, a satchel full of records on his shoulder. Messy hair framing a beautiful face. It's difficult to imagine he once walked the streets with a bald head and eyes without eyebrows. Mine are almost all gone by now. I take another good look at his full eyebrows and long curly lashes. Looks promising. I had no idea that eyebrows have such a significant task in a face. With them nearly gone my face looks like an unfinished painting.

We order mineral water and decide to share an apple pie with whipped cream. The hospital will be happy to see me eating. Anything really; as long as I eat. They don't put much stock in the old saying "You are what you eat." I'm in a constant debate with my nurses because every cancer diet—no matter how much they vary—predicts that cancer feeds on sugar, meaning I avoid sweets as much as possible. But today is an exception. Today is the day I meet Jurriaan.

"Jurriaan—"

"Please, call me Jur."

Must be a fellow-cancer-patient privilege.

"Was it bad?"

"Yeah, you could say that. The chemo wasn't working and neither was the radiation. In the end they managed to contain it."

"Contain it?"

"Yeah. The doctors can't quite explain it ... It just stopped spreading."

"Oh. But is it gone?"

"No, it's still in my body. Like I said, they can't really explain it."

I tell him my diagnosis and what the doctors think my chances are. "I try to take it day by day, but ..."

"Sophie, it's rough, and it's going to be a long process before you get better. You know as well as I do that one good scan doesn't mean you're healed. The best thing you can do is try to find some peace."

"Maybe, but I'm still terrified. Sometimes I can't handle the fear. It gets so overwhelming."

"Don't let the fear get to you. You can't face everything all at once. Try to break up your fear. The fear of being alone, of dying; fear of the pain and of everything you'll miss out on. Just the way you take your illness day by day, face your fears day by day. If you break it down and see each fear for what it is, you can overcome them."

"Did that work for you?"

"Yes, and it will work for you, too. You're strong, anyone can see that. I'm sure you'll get through this." Jur makes it sound so easy. His dark eyes look at me intently. So intently that I lose everything around me and nothing else exists but him.

"You know, you can always call me. Even at night. I know what you're going through."

After two hours Jur is the first to get up to leave. I could have stayed much longer, but I keep that a secret. I watch him as he crosses the now-deserted square. My heart is still beating fast from our conversation. I never expected a cancer buddy to come in such a nice-looking package.In two hours he took away all my loneliness of the past two months. I could eat apple pie à la mode with this guy every day.

MONDAY, APRIL 4

Back in the seventies, my father used his inheritance to purchase a run-down seventeenth-century canal house in Amsterdam. It soon turned out to be a good investment. He moved in with five friends and they all renovated it together, and now each of them has their own tile engraved in the hallway: Ton (my father), Raymond, Henk, Mark, Geert-Jan, and another Ton. Loes, my mother, was the last tile to be added. My parents' romance started just a few houses down from ours, where Mom used to live before my father snatched her away from her basement apartment.

Visitors compare our house to the house where Anne Frank was hidden because of all the stairways and unexpected corners, but it was still just a construction site when they fell in love. The staircases hadn't been built yet, and the house was filled with construction debris. Every night they would climb three stories up ladders to the top floor and fall asleep on a pile of cement bags.

The rest of the group moved out when my mom's first baby bump appeared. Sis came, and three years later I was born, in what is still my parents' bedroom. Sis and I were soon followed by three cats: Keesje, Tiger, and Saartje. Keesje was sent to a "petting zoo" early on. My parents couldn't bear to tell their little girls the truth, even though that cat was meaner than mean. Tiger got run over when he was only three; cause of death: two collapsed kitty lungs. Fifteen-year-old Saartje is the survivor. Her sight isn't as sharp as it used to be, and unfortunately she suffers from dementia, which could explain her poorly calculated attacks on passing Rottweilers.

* * *

Some colors just don't match, but my father's never been able to see that. This morning he pulled on an apple green shirt with an olive green jacket.

"For a special occasion!" he says. Bless him. The occasion in question is dropping me off at the hospital again.

These days he hates to shop; he can't be bothered. But it was different when he was younger. Back then he had a mustache at least twenty centimeters long that curled up at both ends like Dalí's. Before he went to sleep each night he clamped the ends with two clothespins to keep them curled. And when he went to parties he brought his "pet" with him: a stuffed crocodile on roller skates with a leash around its neck. My father pulled him around all night long, dressed in striped boat shirts with an Italian silk scarf around his neck. Both the mustache and the crocodile are gone now, but all the rest has stayed.

When my father met my mother she was still running her antique shop. In the evenings she worked for a fashion designer, sewing costumes and evening dresses. By the time my sister and I were born, she had swapped her fishnet stockings and cowboy boots for pencil skirts and vintage heels. I don't know if it's Amsterdam or them, but I've come to realize that my parents are kind of cool. Nothing's ever been taboo in our house. Although it's easier to talk to my mom about stuff, my father turns everything into a joke, not leaving much untouched either. Like the other day in the hospital when

I went to pee and he waited in the hallway for me, and I discovered my pubic hair was now parting from me too.

"I wonder if they sell bunches of pubic hair at the wig store?" he joked.

"Or maybe they'll throw some in for free with the purchase of a wig?" I replied.

"The colors do need to match of course."

"Of course."

* * *

For the same occasion for which my father wears his green ensemble, I have put Sue on my head and packed Blondie and Daisy—in the hospital I prefer to blend in rather than stand out. I've left Stella home, whom I haven't taken out in months. On the way to the hospital it's always a bit quiet in the car, because we have to prepare ourselves for Dr. L, rhabdomyosarcoma, fear, and all the other misery the hospital has to offer.

But the moment I set foot in the building I switch gears, and the only thing on my list is survival. Despite the ward smelling like chemo and death, I do feel safe in the hospital. It's a small and lonely world but also a cozy and warm one. That switch gets me through my hospital days but makes the distance between my two worlds feel greater than ever. In the hospital I'm a girl too sick for her age, seeing time pass by while lying in bed. But the outside world is so full of life, being so many women at the same time and being occupied with only one thing: having a good time.

Today I get to see the images from my scan. There's a series of small, dark images hanging in front of me that Dr. L has clamped to his projection screen.

Dr. L laughs when I walk into his office as fierce Sue, and then turns to the matter at hand: my lungs. I can see it for myself, the tumors are smaller. The contour of my right lung shows much fewer abnormalities than it did two months ago, when the battle had only just begun. The pleura around my left lung runs in a curve so nice and smooth I could copy it with a compass. The fleece around my right lung, however, is not geometric in the least. It looks like spaghetti with some odd pieces of ravioli. The biggest ravioli is down low, close to my liver. I named the three hanging around the middle of my lung "Huey," "Dewey," and "Louie." There's a loner up at the top, hidden deep behind my right breast. I christened him "Naughty Norbert." "Rhabdo" means rod-shaped, "myo" means muscle tissue, and a "sarcoma" is a malignant growth. In a myosarcoma, the tumor cells attach themselves to the body's soft tissue. It can be connective tissue, muscle tissue, or any other type of tissue. This kind of cancer can occur anywhere in the body but usually occurs in the arms and legs, due to the diagonal tissue that makes up those muscles, and occasionally leads to amputation. I count my lucky stars that my cancer cells are swimming around my lungs.

On the scan the abnormalities are not much bigger than a needle point. In the first scan, the largest tumor was the size of a Ping-Pong ball. Now it's half that. The fact that the tumors are attached to an organ and that that organ is a lung pretty much rules out an operation. That gives me one less weapon to fight with, but there's always radiation.

There are three discernible stages of my disease, and Dr. L tells me I fall in the middle category. Not the toughest group, but not the easiest either. Unfortunately, because my disease is so rare, scientists haven't been able to collect much information on the cause or the recovery process. Most believe it to be caused by an abnormality that developed when I was still just an embryo, but no one can tell me why this abnormality has suddenly decided to try and kill me now, twenty-one years later. In any case, all this has led to plenty of discussion among the pathologists, anatomists, and oncologists at my weekly diagnosis sessions. Apparently, this all-star team doesn't always agree, not even on my diagnosis, but Dr. L tells me I don't need to worry about that too much as long as the treatment is working. Which it is.

My age makes my case a little puzzling too. It's very much a children's disease. Getting through the treatment will be as tough a battle as fighting my disease. Therefore, my blood values are carefully monitored. Blood transfusions for my low red blood cell count, leukocyte injections for my white blood cells, and thrombocyte transfusions to boost my blood count even further. Low blood counts mean no chemo. In real life, I can see it in my pale skin and lack of energy, my weak immune system and the constant bruises all over my body.

When Dr. L is finished, I walk out of his office and let the tension ease out of me. Even though I've been given good news again, Dr. L's office will never be a place I can relax.

I can tell the cure is working, also without the scan. My body is getting used to the new drugs and recovering better after each round of chemo. I'm slowly putting weight back on, and as long as I take my antinausea drugs on time, I no longer have to throw up. Although chemo kills much more than is good for me, I try to see it as a strange rather than poisonous enemy—one who's helping me get better. It's my disease and my battle.

These days I study at the hospital's medical library rather than at the university. Here I can finally face my greatest fears. I carry a copy of my file everywhere. Every doctor who crosses my path is questioned. My nurses spend their coffee breaks making copies of medical journals for me. The once-alien values on my lab form are now familiar and even have the power to comfort me. I want to know and understand and research everything—including my chances of survival, however crude it may be to see my own mortality translated into statistics. The day that it became clear my tumors were attached only to my lung and not my liver, those chances went up from 15 percent to 70 percent. My first CT scan is in the bag. The number of soaked T-shirts beside my bed has been reduced to zero, the visible "raviolis" around my lung to three. I feel stronger, less a victim of my illness. It's not a reality anymore I can't deal with. So I moved back into my own room. Away from my parents' protective bosom, but still within arm's reach.

WEDNESDAY, APRIL 6

My father isn't the only one who has trouble mixing colors. The interior decorators of the hospital must have missed out on their color-matching classes. Apparently the primary colors divided up into square patches on the walls of the pulmonary ward have a psychological meaning. The yellow window frames set off against the blue contours are meant to bring me a sense of peace and calm. I seriously wonder which unrest came first in the days of Dr. K: the one caused by the colors or the one caused by needles. Here on the C6 ward they managed to keep this experimental designer at bay and opted for soft lilac and baby blue, a combination that strongly reminds me of the interior of my primary school. Maybe that interior was meant to calm down its occupants as well.

I call C6 my resort spa, which isn't really that far from the truth. It offers me everything a spa does: peace and quiet, treatments that (hopefully) leave me healthier than when I arrived, and nurses who dote on me hand and foot.

This will be the last of my weekly chemo cocktails. After this stay, I get a new dose only once every three weeks.

Bas is about to call out his usual "Hey, Baldy" when he discovers Sue on my head. "Surprise!" I call out. Nurse Pauke, another nurse, is not amused and immediately gets down to business.

"Heart, bladder, and kidneys: those are the organs we need to keep an eye on. Do you have any complaints?" Her no-nonsense attitude does me well.

"My heart? Well, it could use a bit more romance, but that's probably not what you meant," I answer playfully. "Otherwise, I can't hold my pee in as long as I used to. Sometimes I have some leakage issues ..." I trail off. Bas jokes that he'll find me some Depends for old ladies and leads me to my room.

I've been downgraded to a bed in one of the shared rooms. Until now I'd been protected from this fate. The four private rooms on the ward are reserved for patients who are dying, need to be in isolation, or are otherwise exceptional. I'd fallen into this last category during my previous stays, being the youngest and the most recently diagnosed, but unfortunately there are too many cases in the other two categories at the moment. So, as my condition gets better, I am condemned to a room full of cancer.

Wedged in between Aunt Agony and Auntie Blah, I occasionally exchange knowing glances with my elderly neighbor across the room, who has been the unfortunate witness to their gossipfest for a few days now. The average age in this room must have been about seventy; I brought it down to fifty-eight and a half.

"Good morning! Anybody thirsty?" The ever-cheery coffee lady is making her rounds.

Not a stir.

"Not all at once," she jokes. Still no response; we vegetables are busy vegetating. She fills our tea and coffee mugs all the same. I'm hooked up to my IV pump, and an annoying new nurse is making numerous attempts at taking some blood samples.

Next, the cleaning lady enters to sterilize all the cancer cells floating around the room.

Mom sits in the chair beside my bed. Dear, loyal Mom. Not a day goes by that she doesn't put on her red lipstick, even when she was going in for her own chemo treatments. She's energetic and assertive, especially where her daughter's health is concerned. She barely gives the interns the time of day, and even the residents are given a hard time every now and then.

"Are you sure about that? Does Dr. L know about this?" is one of her favorite lines. Or when my IV is being changed: "Only if you can manage it in one go. Otherwise you can go and get your supervisor." She guards my bed like a knight guards his castle. We share a lot in this awkward space. She sees exactly how my mouth stiffens when the IV is inserted and how my smile disappears when I'm sick to my stomach. When the hospital sucks and all the people in it are assholes. Sometimes that's all it is. And she knows that. But having her in arm's reach is as comforting as it's difficult. When I'm alone, the illness is like a problem I just have to go through. With my mother sitting next to me, it's not just my problem anymore. And that makes it too big a problem to handle. I don't have room for my family's emotions, only for my own. Seeing them stiffen in fear or break down in sorrow is more than I can deal with. My family knows. They are in constant careful anticipation of my emotional and physical state of being. Also, the continuous fatigue can turn me into a real sour prune. Whenever anyone comes near me on a bad day, they hold their breath for fear of irritating the princess on the pea.

* * *

Dr. L stops by. As usual his esteemed interns accompany him so they can discuss their latest medical discoveries during lunch; cancer-talk while they chow down their cheeseburgers. Dr. K appears only in my dreams, and every so often in the corridors of the hospital when I'm on my way to visit Dr. L. It's not fair, really, that of all the doctors in all the different specialties in this hospital, the one I ended up with has the worst bedside manner.

"There you are. It's always a bit of a hunt to find you. Is this your latest addition?"

Hmmm. What's that? A joke? I swapped wigs about an hour ago. I nod proudly. "Her name is Blondie."

Sue and Daisy are hanging over the IV pole, which I have taken to using as a clothes hanger. It also sports a dressing gown and my purse. The interns giggle in chorus. Even Dr. L gives me a brief smirk. Something's changing about him. He makes jokes now. And he looks at me differently. In a kind and caring way.

Although the basis for our interaction is purely medical, our relationship feels extremely personal. At least to me. The hours I share with Dr. L are the most intimate moments of my life, given they are the most painful. He is with me when all my defenses are down. He knows the fear I feel when he looks concerned and the joy I experience when he gives me good news. I can't fight this fight without him. And I don't want to, anymore.

Now that I've seen his kindness, I wonder what he puts on his sandwiches. And what sort of house he wakes up in. And how he gets from that house to the hospital. So far I've found out that he lives in a village whose name starts with an O and that he takes the train there and back. I find that strange.

This man is so immensely important to me that I expected him to travel in a chauffeured car with tinted windows and a butler. Not to have a chaotic morning ritual like us mortals of making the kids' sandwiches, gathering papers, and rushing late out the door, off to the hospital to save lives.

I spend all morning lying in bed while the busy stream of traffic continues around me. It's only the first day, but I'm fed up already. I'm smelly, dizzy, and feeling bitter thinking about the plans I have or had. I wonder if it's easier to know if it's the present tense or the past than not knowing at all.

THURSDAY, APRIL 7

All the perfumes and lotions in the world can't counteract the inescapable BO caused by chemo. Even my pee stinks. "Chemo pee," Pauke calls it. I'm reminded of the smell all day long, seeing as how I have to use a bedpan instead of a proper adult toilet. At first I tried to get rid of the stink with all of the contents of my toiletry bag, but I've since learned that I don't stand a chance against it.

Pauke, who wears Birkenstocks as if they were designed for her, has just stopped by to weigh me and take my temperature and blood pressure. She's not like the other nurses; she's not like some of the others a deejay, a part-time salesperson, or a hip young thing. She's an old-fashioned nurse who likes to get things done. She's so tall that as she works her way efficiently from bed to bed, she reminds me of Miss Clavel from the Madeline books I adored as a child. She makes sure that everything that needs to happen gets done but never loses her cheerful smile—even when her needle misses its target every now and then, but that only happens on her off days, which even *she* apparently has.

Today I'm in too crappy a mood to wander the corridors of my ward. After a few hours of chemo the nausea slowly starts to rise. It's not enough to make me throw up but more than enough to make me shudder at the thought of eating. Pauke coaxes me into getting out of bed long enough for her to change the sheets. She does this every day, unless I win her over with an extra-sad face. I've only managed that once, when I timed it perfectly so that I threw up just as she came into the room.

I ask her if she ever thinks of me when she disappears into her own world after she leaves the hospital at the end of her shift.

"Yes," she says, "but when I think about you I think of figs and dates, not IVs or sterile needles." She thinks of delicious, sweet figs and soft, creamy dates. Just because I once read the nutritional values of these fruits out loud while she was taking my blood pressure. That's another way of looking at things.

So when I think of Pauke outside of the hospital, I think of her three teenagers at home waiting for her to finish her shift; of Cap Ferrat, because she has the most beautiful stories about it; and of Miss Clavel.

And when the moment comes that she disappears into her world, I change wigs in order to not disappear in mine. I take off Daisy and put on Blondie. Her magic is at its most powerful in the moment of transformation. Then I fall asleep with my short blonde bob glued to my skull, dancing the night away to the sounds of my tall friend standing next to me and with Mr. Gatsby himself, in his royal back garden and lifted by his royal heart, into a different life, leaving mine behind.

FRIDAY, APRIL 8

In the morning I'm woken up by a nasty lady with an even nastier-looking needle in her hand. She's lugging around a plastic bin with all her equipment. It's not even eight o'clock; my face is still stuck to my pillow, and I refuse to open my eyes. I'm so nauseous. Resistance is futile, so I meekly stick out my arm. I keep one eye open and focus hard on her needle in the hope that she gets it right in one go. No such luck. *Jerk*.

She draws aside the curtain and I'm served my breakfast.

"Morning!" the coffee lady calls out so that anyone still asleep is now definitely awake. Just like every other morning, she brings me a thermos of boiling water so that I can make my own green medicinal tea. I realize I need to pee when I see a new bag of salt solution being pumped into my drip, but that means messing around with my tubes. I wish I could just go back to bed, but the constant stream of coffee ladies, needles, nurses, and doctors makes it impossible for me to close my eyes and pretend that I'm somewhere else.

I get up and ready myself to go see the dental hygienist. I have to see him pretty regularly to make sure my teeth don't fall out from all the medicines running through me. So far they're holding up pretty well. According to him I have strong teeth. "Just like your mother."

To get to his office I have to venture down to where the normal people are. Normal people who might have minor ailments but aren't rotting away upstairs. Normal people who are just here for appointments, not to stay. Downstairs everything is still innocent.

Chained to my IV stand, I take the elevator to the ground floor. In an attempt to blend in, I've put on my normal, everyday clothes: jeans and a black turtleneck sweater, Blondie on my head. Too bad I can't hide my bright red puffy cheeks. It feels as if everyone is looking at me. Their looks tell me that they know I haven't come from just any ward, but from the oncology department, where the people with cancer are kept. These confrontations are maybe the worst part of the whole disease. For them it's unreal and for me it's reality. It's in their eyes, in their way of looking at me; I see I'm not one of them anymore.

When my visit to the dentist is done, I go back upstairs as quickly as possible.

* * *

My IV is like a guardian, always by my side: when the lights go out and I wash my face, brush my teeth, fall asleep, and dream of Dr. K. But also when the lights come back on and I wake up, wash my face, brush my teeth, and eat my breakfast. We are connected by a thin and softly pulsing tube that carries a gentle stream of fluids between us. He never leaves me to sleep or eat and he never needs to rest from carrying my medicines around. Most of the time we don't speak, but when he senses danger he makes himself heard and brings the nurses running to my side.

Although I can't avoid loneliness when evening sets in, these are the most precious moments of my day. I'm finally left alone to lose myself in my thoughts, to stare out the window, or to watch *Desperate Housewives*, occasionally joined by the nurses who stop by to catch a minute of easy amusement. Every night before closing my eyes, I look at the clock tower next to the hospital. From Dr. K's office in the pulmonary ward I saw the same clock from a different angle. It's been a strange journey from that ward to this one. Time is unfamiliar to me now, but the clock keeps ticking just the same.

Oh, Dr. K. I still hope for an unexpected visit from him, or a kiss, or a card. At night my loneliness reaches fever pitch, and my longing for his strong shoulders is the worst. I truly believe it's his arms I long for, not those of a nice, uncomplicated twentysomething. I hate the thought of dying without having known true love. If I die tomorrow, the church will be crowded with plenty of flings, but there's none I would call right now.

Farther down the hall someone is dying, and it sounds like a rhino with a toothache. They might have warned me, so I could have ordered some earplugs. *Will I sound like that? Or smell like that?* What a nightmare. *Please don't let it be me.* I push the red button and soon Bas arrives with some earplugs. Even at three A.M. it's nice to see him approaching my bed. The earplugs are pink and moldable. As I warm them up between my fingers, I hear a low threatening whisper in the dark.

"Shut your face!" One of my ward companions has also reached the end of his rope. Sometimes this place really is a nuthouse.

When I fall asleep my cheeks are wet. At least I get to go home tomorrow and eat my favorite dish: Mam's homemade soto ayam.

MONDAY, APRIL 11

It is week eleven of my chemo and week two of the new term at university. I've been enrolled throughout my treatment; the mention of the words "cancelation of enrollment" was just too much of cancellation in once.

In the name of moving on I've picked up my books again. For obvious reasons I've fallen behind, all this time I have left my books untouched. When I enrolled in political science at the time, it wasn't so much for the politics, or the sake of studying. I enrolled for the life I wanted to live after: roaming the planet with a degree in development studies. Roaming the planet has always been highest on my list.

In the summer after my high school graduation I bought a ticket to Tibet. My interest in that country began somewhere between the novels of Hermann Hesse and an intense crush on a guy named Ralph, whose house was covered with Tibetan prayer flags. Since the age of fourteen I had dreamed of wandering the world by myself, and I figured I would be most by myself in the Himalayan plateau of Tibet. Finally, at eighteen, graduated and free, the only way to get around there was if I went with an organized group trip. When I got to the airport, ready to start my grand adventure, I saw my travel companions were a bunch of retirees. That moment sort of killed my dream (and my self-image), but it turned out that the longer I traveled with them the more adventurous I felt. My older companions had been traveling the whole world for years and seen parts of it that I never would. They actually gave me a sense of home. During grad school my dream to leave home and wonder around by myself in Tibet, had been a strange one. But now I was surrounded by fellow dreamers.

The trip began in Beijing and ended a month later in Kathmandu, where I decided to stick around a little longer. Suddenly I was really on my own. Although the first hours were great, prospering in my new freedom, it sucked big time when night came. I think this was the first time I experienced loneliness. Sitting on my bed, so far away from home, in a place I didn't know, life seemed suddenly quite simple. I understood I had two options: staying in and feeling lonely or going out and living my dream.

I found a room with only a bed and a small table in a small hostel for backpackers in the neighborhood. Everyday I walked the streets of Kathmandu and soon collected some travel buddies, including a German girl named Silvi with whom I completed the Annapurna Circuit. We spent three weeks hiking and talking while being amazed of the beauty of the Himalayas. We climbed up to 5,400 meters, sleeping in small guesthouses that hardly kept us warm. The frigid winds blew right through the wooden walls. It was so cold at night that we slept with our hats and gloves on. As two girls traveling alone, we had one rule: if one of us had to pee at night, the other had to go too. I remember realizing that it was just as cold inside as outside while squatting together in the middle of the night, awed by the icy summits surrounding us as we tried not to splash on our shoes and legs.

After two months in Nepal I said good-bye to Silvi and drifted on to India. It was India that stole my heart twice. First the country, then a man named Sanjay. We roamed the streets together, and I soaked in the dirt and beauty, marveling at the colors and contrasts. When I came home I decided to major in political science and development studies.

Now, back at university we discuss the schedule for the coming semester. Right away I'm given a date to present my paper—the same week that I'm supposed to be admitted to the hospital for my next chemo session. I look around me as I listen to the professor go over the syllabus. It's confusing to be here. Not just because I don't understand all the terms swimming around on the board in front of me, but also because, looking at the students around me, I can't fool myself as I can sitting in a café with one of my wigs: it's clear that I'm not like them anymore. They are here preparing themselves for tomorrow, while all I can think about is the day at hand. The biggest trouble of having cancer is not physical. It is not being allowed anymore to think of the life you're going to be living after finishing your studies. And that kind of kills all my ambition to be here in the first place.

I tug at Blondie—she's the only way I can reappear at school without having to answer too many questions. I'm here to ask the questions, not answer them. But wearing Blondie as an attempt to pass as the old me makes one thing cruelly clear: the old me, studying for a grand life, dating until I found the right one, carelessly getting drunk, she doesn't exist anymore. In my new life, wearing a wig and being anonymous is liberating. Wearing a wig in class is the contrary, a painful reminder of who I can no longer be.

When class is finished I pack my books, with no plans to unpack them for a very long time. It hurts but it's also freeing. Maybe I simply don't *have* to anymore. Don't have to contemplate my career, don't have to become someone important, don't have to learn things for later. I just have to get through the day. Why study for a future that might turn out completely different? Better to focus on the present, which I know is real. It's time for some reflection. Time to get up close and personal. Starting with my very own scalp. I'm still hiding her.

TUESDAY, APRIL 12

Although everything is different, some things really do never change. Like peeing in the shower. I love stepping into a warm shower in the morning and letting it all go. Yesterday I ate asparagus and was reminded of that in the shower this morning. Beyond that, though, a morning ritual is something I've never known. The secrets behind all those colour tablets and the proper makeup techniques have always been a mystery to me. I can barely manage mascara on a regular basis. Let alone nail polish. I used to like to spend my mornings in a café with the newspaper and a coffee.

But that was then.

Now I've become one of those women who have exchanged the au naturel look for powders and brushes. I start with my eyebrows. I was born with full, bushy brows, but now they are completely gone. With my special brush—which cost me forty-two euros!—I carefully color in where I think my arches used to be. Next up is eyeliner. There are no eyelashes left to lengthen, but eyeliner helps create the illusion. When the painting and coloring is done I look to my wigs. Stella is not an option; she looks as cancerous as my bald head. Which leaves Daisy, Sue, or Blondie. But for some reason they won't do today. I want to be someone else. Someone bold, someone from a faraway country, someone unknown.

I gulp down the last of my tea, take my bike, and park it ten minutes later in front of the door of my favorite store.

I'm starting to enjoy this metamorphosis game. Shopping at the theater-supply store is not that different from shopping at H&M. I need a hairdo with a long fringe to cover the skin where my eyebrows once were. In a corner I see a Mia Wallace—Uma Thurman in *Pulp Fiction*—look-alike. I try it on. The cut is exactly what I need. The black color is too severe for me, but luckily she comes in different colors. In an auburn tan she works wonders on my pale skin. The long strands fall over my shoulders, while the fringe covers part of my eyes.

"We can easily adjust that for you, just a little trim."

"How much is this one?" I ask.

"Fifty-two fifty."

I look up in surprise. This is by far the cheapest wig I have gotten so far. Who would have thought that Uma, aka Miss Mia Wallace, would be so affordable?

Beside me a dark-skinned woman is trying on wigs too, but for funnier reasons than cancer. I hear her talking about a fancy party. She tucks her Afro under a shiny white bob. The synthetic glow almost hurts my eyes, but the effect is amazing.

"Could I try that one as well?" I ask. Although the color works differently on my skin than it does on hers, I immediately love the wig. She makes me look like an outsider, something I've been fighting against ever since I got sick. But she also seems like someone who doesn't care that she is. And on the spot, wearing her, I don't either. I call her Platina.

"That'll be fifty-two fifty plus sixty-six ... one-eighteen fifty. The hair spray is on the house, for preferred customers." The salesman winks at me.

I walk out wearing Platina. It doesn't get more obvious than this. With Platina, I'm not hiding, I'm showing off. I never thought I'd find wearing a wig fun, but it is. Six wigs, six names, six times as many friends and admirers. Six subcharacters, and behind each of them a little piece of Sophie. An insecure Sophie: Stella. A sensual Sophie: Uma. A headstrong Sophie: Sue. A thoughtful Sophie: Blondie. A fun-loving Sophie: Platina. A romantic Sophie: Daisy. All my wigs make me feel like more of a woman and less of a girl. Maybe that's why I like them so much. Today, as Platina, I feel different than yesterday, when I was Blondie. Sue gets people's attention, but she also makes me feel more headstrong, more confident even. Sue's red hair makes people think I'm a sassy broad when I walk into the room. And suddenly the clumsiness that comes with being somewhere between a girl and a woman doesn't exist. As Sophie I can feel insecure, but as Sue nobody can bring me down. I proudly examine my fake but fabulous new look in every window. I hop on my bike and head off to meet Jan and Rob at the pub. I can spot their grins a mile off. Nobody can see Platina and not smile. Jan loves crazy and kooky, and Rob loves me. As Platina, I'm a bit of both.

* * *

On the Gravenstraat, one of Amsterdam's main drags, I wear Uma to meet up with the boys—Jan, Jochem, and Rob—for lunch. Jan and I have had the same routine since I got cancer. Although he gets up much earlier than I do, we always eat together. He has lunch while I have brunch. After a circuit of the farmers' market to pick up some fresh asparagus, we split up. As a successful television presenter and a part-time active gay who enjoys his own company best, Jan disappears to his writing room. I do the same. The words keep on coming; my journal is starting to take on some serious heft. Rob, a freelance cameraman, has the same relaxed schedule as Jan and me—as long as he's not called for a last-minute shoot or to fill in for someone. The least successful of the bunch is Jochem, who keeps himself so extraordinarily busy doing nothing that he seems to have a busier existence than my doctor. He's constantly fixated on where he isn't rather than where he is—worried that he's going to miss out on something. Looking at him today, I realize I was just like him. Cancer did its spell.

I meet up with the boys nearly every day. Over wine, french fries, and cigarettes (for them), the first fun has come back into my life. I can never keep it dry when Jan does his impression of Rob at the gym.

Jan tells us he's been writing about those first days after I got my diagnosis, when we walked, dazed and confused, around the city. Along with the rest of our gang, Rob and Jan abandoned their other obligations for a few days. It helps to know that we were all consumed by confusion then—that I wasn't alone even though it sometimes felt that way. Maybe that's why it's so good when we're together. We share the same fear, the same powerlessness, and we cry the same tears.

These moments together have made me a different person. Someone who is present at the place she's at. It's new for me to abandon my rush to see everything, without losing my ability to discover new things. I no longer allow myself to look too far ahead at internships for my résumé, trips I want to take, books I have to read. I seize all I can. I seize not only the day, I seize my breakfasts, my cups of tea, the occasional glass of wine, my afternoons outside in the sun or snuggled up inside when it rains. I seize the evening sun and the thunderstorms;

I seize and seize some more. My jam-packed agenda has made way for blank pages that are filled with all these seized moments. And I love it.

Rob interrupts my thoughts. "Hey, sexy, your hairdo is perfect just like that. You look gorgeous. Really." A smile spreads from one side of my face all the way to the other. Rob and I may just be friends, but we've been crazy about each other from day one. I always reach out for his hand when we're walking the streets together. We're always laughing, with or without Jan. And we both get a little jealous when the other flirts with the next table over on the terrace. I'd say we belong to each other a little bit.

"Well, my dear, you certainly haven't lost your wild streak, have you?" one of the older regulars calls out. Apparently Rob is not the only one who fancies Uma.

Cheekily, I join in the game and toss around my hair. Jan smiles at me while watching the scene vigilantly. Although I attract more attention as a blonde, the impression that Uma makes is incredible. It helps to know that it's nothing more than an act, a break from being a cancer patient. I wonder what the guy at the bar would say if I paraded in with my bald scalp. Nothing much, surely.

So much has changed in my life, and so much in me. A strange face in the mirror's reflection. I hardly recognize my old self, with or without a wig. Too much distance between us. It does help, dressing up as all these different personalities, to learn how to see myself. Like, that's me, and that's me, and that's also me. I feel almost lucky that I can wear different wigs and try out different personalities. That I can somehow figure out who I am underneath.

FRIDAY, APRIL 15

"Sophie!"

I'm standing in front of Hildus's front door. Just as I go to ring the bell I hear someone shout my name.

With a bag full of groceries, Hildus approaches me, looking at me searchingly. "Yes, it is you. Did you get a haircut?"

Assuming he hasn't heard, I play along. "Yeah," I say, and conjure up a doubtful smile. A poor effort. Hildus doesn't look convinced. His eyes are fixed on my wig, Blondie, which moves about as naturally as Dolly Parton's.

I'm on a date. Dating with cancer is quite scary. The last time I flirted with the opposite sex was in New York at the New Year's Eve party with Annabel. But since my diagnosis, I haven't bothered with guys and they haven't bothered with me. Hildus and I last saw each other at a party in December, before I left for New York. When we run into each other we always flirt, update each other's numbers, and promise to get in touch. That promise has never been fulfilled, until recently when he sent me a text out of the blue.

I bumped into The Ex at that same party. We were together for a year and spent most of that year in each other's company. Being ten years apart, we had different lives but we shared as much as we could. Jogging in the morning, eating breakfast, checking our e-mails before running off to work or class. He started work at ten thirty in his gallery, and I had my first class at eleven. That half hour gave me just enough time to make it to the university from his house. It's odd how close we started and how far apart we ended up.

Since then, it's been radio silence. I had secretly hoped that my cancer might elicit some sign of life from him—a call, a card, hell, even a text message would have been nice. But nothing. The strange thing is that he already lost an ex-girlfriend to cancer. This comforts me in a way, makes me think I've got good chances. I mean, how likely is it that he will lose another one to cancer? I want to tell him I'm okay, that I still eat, laugh, and bike through town when the weather allows it. That I'm living like a normal person, more or less. And maybe that I'm dating again. Sort of.

"Actually, your hair looks kind of ... wiggish," Hildus says as we climb the stairs to his flat. Coming from someone who doesn't know anything about my illness, this is quite a downer. Wiggish. So, Hildus thinks my new do looks "wiggish." *Ouch.* I'd opted for Blondie because she looks the most like the old me. Blondie instantly deflates from "ready to hit the town" to a sad little pile of peroxide strands. I've spent at least three days styling the wig in preparation for this date. I guess I overdid it.

I feel naked—worse, transparent. There's no more sign of Blondie, it's just me with a wig on my head. I look at the stairs. I consider running back down them as fast as possible. But I swallow the lump in my throat and keep on climbing.

Hildus's living room looks like a jungle. There are plants all over the place. Every time I turn my head there are leaves dangling in my face. I'm terrified Blondie will get stuck on a branch in the apartment, and I fidget nervously. I try to hide my discomfort with an awkward giggle. I came prepared to swoon—I even attached a special tape to the inside of Blondie just to be sure.

I guess that was a bit too much to ask for.

Hildus tells me what it is that he's actually "doing": part-time surfer, television entertainer, and writer. Pretty much everything that sounds interesting. While he's going on about his grand life, I'm trying to hide my lack of one.

"Want some wine?" *Wine? Hmmm. Except for two glasses I haven't had a drop of alcohol since the news. I better stick to juice.*

"No, thanks. Do you have tomato juice?" Wow, that must sound awkward.

"Oh, uh, sure. I think I do."

I follow him into the kitchen, where Hildus comes up close behind me. He puts his hands around my waist.

"Let's eat first," I hear myself mumble. *Nice one, Blondie. Is that all you've got?*

He takes two vegetarian sausages out of their packaging while he explains the importance of nature and eating organically. "Are you aware of all the crap you put in your body? Or how we treat animals for slaughter?" I pretend to be reading the interminable list of ingredients on the package so as not to roll my eyes. He doesn't know half of what I'm aware of. Mr. Dilletante, dabbling in veggie sausages, and bad ones at that.

I escape to the living room and sit down on the couch. Hildus walks in with two plates and sits down next to me. The food looks awful and impossible to swallow without some help. I'm all about health, I have to, but this is just a no-go. "Do you have any ketchup?"

After dinner, Hildus slides in closer to me on the couch, his hands moving toward my face. He's making the move. I freeze. *Do I want this?* I guess this means I'm still desirable, so that's good news. And apparently my wig has passed the test. Slowly I feel Blondie coming back to me. *Thank you, Maybelline.* Completely tense, I move a few inches away on the dusty old couch, just out of his reach. Hildus, like most men, doesn't get the message. He curls up beside me and starts running his hands through my hair, something Blondie is not at all prepared for nor would ever accept. Just before it all goes awry, I duck away.

Hildus looks at me with an expression of surprise and confusion.

"I think I have to tell you something," I say.

Hildus is silent.

"I'm sick. I have cancer. You're right about the wig. I'm totally bald."

Hildus is still silent. But he doesn't look shocked.

I wait a few seconds for him to speak. Nothing.

"That's why I've been acting so awkward." Nothing. "You're so quiet. Are you shocked?"

"No, not really. I mean, yes, of course, this is a big deal, but I don't care. I still want to kiss you."

"Oh? What about the wig? And my bald head? And that I might die?"

"You're still Sophie."

Silence, this time on my part. And then a smile. I suddenly realize it's what I really came for. I lean over and kiss Hildus, grateful and passionate all at once.

Then I get up, ready to go.

"Don't you want to stay over?"

"No."

"Why not?"

"Because I'm bald. It just doesn't feel right anymore, to cuddle up with all this baggage, visible or not. I would rather lie in bed with my cat."

"Just stay for a little bit."

"No." I look at him. "I can't and I don't want to, but thank you for this evening." I give him a last kiss, get up, and walk to the door. Outside I take a deep breath. My face is all smile. I'm still attractive. I'm still in the game. For a moment I'm back to being a normal girl.

THURSDAY, MAY 19

The shock I went through in January made me forget so many things. I can't remember much of the months before I was told I had cancer. There are people I've met I don't recall, dinners that are a complete blur. It all seems so far away. On the other hand, I remember every detail of the last four months. Maybe this explains why Jur has become such an important figure in my thoughts in such a short period of time.

It's like he's guiding me without even being by my side. I wish we'd see more of each other. I seize every opportunity to meet, but the rules of love are unfortunately not very different now than they were before. After every attempt from my side to be in touch, I patiently wait for him to reach out to me. And unfortunately that can take weeks.

Jur is convinced that meditating helped him survive. I guess when doctors give up on you and you drift off to the land of Buddha with only one mantra—*I will not die*—and you come back more alive than ever, that makes sense. But it makes me restless; I can't sit still on that cushion for more than ten minutes. Jur says I shouldn't worry. That my writing is my meditation. I tried to look as smart as I could, only to hide that I had no idea what to think of that. My writing my meditation? All I can say is that I've come to do only the things that make me happy.

It's week sixteen and my fourth hospital stay has begun. Things are moving quickly, especially when I remember that in two months' time I won't have to spend any more weeks rotting away here. I hardly dare think that this nightmare will soon be a memory. In two months, the first twenty-seven weeks will be over, and I'll only have to come for outpatient treatments once a week. Coming and going on the same day—what bliss.

The sun is shining. Even on C6. I'm cheerful. Besides a cancer diet book, I've also brought along Primo Levi. Such fun. When I open the book, a card falls out with a poem written on it. It's "Ithaka" by C. P. Cavafy. On the back is a letter from Jaap, my loyal and only friend from university, who was never too busy to explain to me—again and again—the most recent statistics.

Dear Sophie,

This is C. P. Cavafy's poem "Ithaka." Read it when you feel sad or afraid. I don't know if it will cheer you up, but it doesn't have to. It teaches you to appreciate life; how it was, how it is, and what to do with it. When you read it, think of ancient Greece, the land of Homer and Socrates, the land where reflecting on destiny and wisdom went hand in hand. Above all, think of the origin of your name: the Sophists were the first ones who weren't satisfied with accepting their destiny—they tried to understand what to do with it.

That is what you must do as well. It is up to you to get better!

Love,

Jaap

Encouraging thought while lying chained to an IV. I watch the comings and goings of white coats: nurses, interns, resident doctors, and, at the top of the food chain, Dr. L, my own medicine man. Some days life in the hospital closely resembles a slapstick comedy. As a patient, I can clearly see the difference between the experienced lifesavers and the rookies. I eavesdrop on the conversations among the nurses, which keep me up to date on all the gossip and intrigues, most of which I exaggerate in my mind to keep me entertained.

"How was your weekend? Were you on duty?"

"Yeah, but not here. I was deejaying at Paradiso." Nurse Esther spins records at local clubs when she's not busy pampering us.

"Oh, meet any cute guys?," the other nurse asks.

"Well, do you remember Gerard? He was here with a seminoma." A tumor in his balls. "He was dancing right in front of my booth. Very cute."

Nice. I tell her that will be me next week, swinging my blonde curls around.

It kind of sucks when you have nothing to add to the conversation. I remember that from the visits to my aunt, who had spent too many years of her life in the hospital. There I was *en famille*, keeping up a poor conversation in a failed attempt to overcome the distance between the patient's bed and the visitor's chair. Uncomfortable, embarrassed. What to say? Where to look? Once people enter this building for unlucky reasons, you lose conversation: they live in a different reality, where other things matter.

Now that person is me. I have come to know that the patients feel the least uncomfortable. I feel bad for my visitors, spending their spare hours at my bedside, robbed of their well-deserved lunch break in the sun. "Is it nice out?" Or when it's raining: "Pouring down, is it?" in my most cheerful and sociable voice.

That's why I ask only a few people to visit me in the hospital, rather than asking everyone to stop by to help kill the time. Nervousness and awkwardness around me only gives me a headache. I'd rather be alone and let my mind wander, like Jur, who lay in a similar bed and had similar thoughts. He vomited bucketfuls. I pass the time in a more productive way: I write, read, polish my nails and, if I'm lucky, receive visits from a doctor with a name starting with *K* and a stethoscope.

I don't need a lot of fellow victims to commiserate with. No roomful of baldies, or a weekend of reflection and meditation in a spiritual castle out in the country with all those scalps and wigs. I prefer the peace and the silence of my own thoughts, where I have apple pie with Jur every day. I have visited a number of websites, though. Websites about cancer—mostly about young people with cancer. It can be lonely having cancer all by yourself. Everyone carries on doing those things that, until recently, were important and significant to you as well. And now here I am, shifting my suddenly secondary cares and concerns aside while trying to survive.

One little bubbling tube.

FRIDAY, MAY 20

"Here she is. What do you want now? Come to bother Dr. L with more of your questions? And who's this you've brought along? Is this your new man?" Nurse Esther stands up from behind her desk, smiling.

I turn around and see a gray and wrinkled C6 patient behind me, who by the looks of things doesn't have much time left. A bundle of laughs, Esther. I once asked Dr. L whether it helped my case that I wasn't as wretched-looking as most of the other C6 prisoners, despite my uncertain prognosis. He told me it did.

Going through chemo is a strange process. It wears me out, but so does the cancer. At least knowing the chemo is killing the tumors manages to energize me at the same time. On my strong days, wearing a wig to match my mood, nobody on the street notices anything out of the ordinary. Besides the massive fatigue I feel after a week of chemo and my hair-free existence, I appear quite healthy. On my low days, my sickness shows on my face, but those are the days that I hide in my bed.

I'm now so familiar here that I always have a good time with the nurses, who know how to make me laugh. I dropped by to kill some of the boredom of my fourth hospital week, immediately forgetting my surroundings when Esther starts telling me about her latest embarrassing escapade, falling backward, camera and all, into the fountain of the Alhambra in Granada.

Pulling my IV pole back to my ward, I pass the door to the hospital chapel and decide to pay a call to Jesus, just to say hi. At least he's always home. These days I regularly stop in for a church visit. Not for some hypocritical idea of finally putting effort into my relationship with God, but honestly, just to pass time. I see Jesus looking down on us from the high beams of the white chapel. Quietly, so as not to disturb the peace, I walk up to him to light a candle for the general good of the world. As well as one for my trusty IV pole: Jesus's heavy eyes seem to tell me lighting a candle for myself is not done. Needing a quick rest, I take a seat on one of the white benches inside. As an atheist or agnostic, I'm still contemplating, praying isn't really my thing. I stare ahead and sink into beautiful thoughts about Dokter K, until my IV rudely bleeps me back to reality. Obediently, I get up and go in search of the nearest electrical socket in the corridor. I maneuver my pole into the right position and come to a halt again.

When I'm sufficiently charged for another walk, I wander toward the Muslim prayer room. It's a free country, and Friday is the first day of the Muslim weekend anyway. I clumsily tie my cardigan over my head and I get down on my knees. Who knows, maybe this will bring me amazing new insights. So far the only insight it's ever brought me is it's not a good time to lose your headscarf, which happened to me once in Iran, while traveling there with a friend. Less common a destination than India or Tibet I guess, but for me it wasn't. Both my parents had visited the country, my mother had even lived in Tehran for two years as a young girl, when the shah was still in power. It turned out a beautiful trip and a very surprising experience: most people we met were not that different to us. Just their regime was.

The day I left, my father gave me a poem about a gardener in Isfahan and told me he'd searched for him close to the famous bridge but never found him. When I set off, I decided I would look for him and bring back the picture he had never been able to shoot. I must have gone on the right day, because when we went to Isfahan I came across a gardener and took his picture to send to my dad.

My IV battery gives up yet again, and as the mosque doesn't appear to be vanquishing my boredom, I leave the quiet room behind and slowly make my way back to C6, like a disciple back to her master.

The elevator comes to a halt on the second floor and the doors open. To my delight, my favorite white coat appears: Dr. K. *Now, that's what I call a sign from God.* He looks at me with a friendly and somewhat cheeky look in his eyes. He comes and stands close behind me, even though we only have to share the cavernous space with two cackling nurses. I hear the nurses chatting about the upcoming staff party this weekend and wonder if Dr. K will be attending and what he wears outside of office hours. I probably like him better in uniform.

On the way up I can feel his breath on my neck. I break out in a light sweat: on my back, under my arms, between my fingers. Three months ago my tumors were causing my sweats; now it's my unceasing crush on Dr K. The elevator comes to a standstill again, this time on the third floor, and the door opens to let out the cackling nurses. I'm starting to recognize them from the many times I've traveled these halls. My typical route takes me first past radiology, then to cardiology via the newborns, then past the operation rooms, then comes my ward: oncology. Before, when I was still in the caring hands of Dr. K I would pass further up through neurology, to the pulmonary and orthopedic wings on the eighth floor—Dr. K's domain.

The nurses disappear around the corner and the knot in my stomach tightens. I have three floors to go, Dr. K another five. With a little luck the elevator will maintain its usual glacial pace, which means another two minutes. Two minutes alone with Dr. K, behind closed doors. I can still feel his breath. Goose bumps on my neck. Everything inside of me is aglow. Here I am in the middle of my ultimate doctor fantasy and I'm paralyzed.

We stand next to each other somewhat awkwardly. It's he who finally breaks the silence by asking after the state of my body, in particular my lung. "You gave us quite a fright, you know."

I smile shyly. Although Daisy falls dramatically around my shoulders, I feel the opposite of sexy with all the fresh chemo pumping through my body. "My oncologist is not the most charming of men," I say.

Dr. K laughs kindly and assures me I am in good hands with Dr. L. "And I've kept my eye on you."

"Will you come and visit me sometime?" I ask. The elevator is slowing down. He nods. Being this close to him, I feel like I'm flying through all sorts of strange worlds.

Ding.

The doors open and I awaken from my fantasy to the eternal boredom of my ward. SIXTH FLOOR—ONCOLOGY stares at me through the open elevator doors. I'm back in my reality: the emaciated-bodies-and-baldies department. I leave Dr. K behind, with a warm glow and a spring in my step.

SATURDAY, MAY 21

My hospital week is over and the sun is shining. I don't have to open my eyes to see that; the heat is burning right through my eyelids. I open my eyes and look at the time on my cell phone, which I fell asleep with last night: half past twelve! The colors through my window are calling out for me to get up.

It's so nice being woken up by the bright sunshine, or by a soft rain that drips me out of my sleep instead of alarm clocks. There's a funny game going on with time today. The same day that she's started walking away from me, leaving me behind with Damocles's sword, she has become very generous with me, giving me for each minute two. No more to-do lists, appointments, even meetings for drinks, but long minutes of warming my face in the first strokes of daylight. Peace has set in. There's a surprisingly close connection between cancer and life.

I get in the shower and lather my whole body in soap. No rush. With curiosity, I study my shower curtain. It's covered in old-school bathing beauties, all with different boobs and butts. I examine my own breasts. Small and round, with tucked-in nipples. Thinking I had a problem, I always played with them to get them to pop out, until I learned there are more women than just me walking around with ice cubes. I find a match with the long, curly-haired girl; she's holding her arms up in the air and pointing her chin down. I turn the water to cold and wait a few moments, for circulation and nipples.

After doing my makeup, I stick my arms up high and jut out my right hip in the mirror. I see the girl from the shower curtain. Today I decide that I'm Daisy: light and full of life.

I fry an egg and stand in front of the stove to watch it bubble. I see how the egg slowly turns bright yellow and white. Multitasking is a thing of the past. After I polish off the last of my egg, I call Rob. No one answers. He must be filming. Annabel does answer and we agree to meet for tea at Café Finch. Finch is that kind of café where you can hang around on your own with a laptop, meet up with friends in a rainy afternoon or go out on a Thursday night and meet someone cute.

That gives me plenty of time to e-mail Dr. L about the status of my stabbing pains and tingling—I can't distinguish the stabs that are getting rid of the tumors from the stabs that are caused by them—and go in search of a solution for my pasty white arms, legs, and cheeks. I have to protect myself from the sun these days, which is not great for someone with a naturally pale complexion. Of course it's better to be pasty than have dark spots all over from the chemo, but there must be some product out there to make me look less sickly. The wigs only do so much.

Out on the street, there are people everywhere—strolling, shopping—all taking their sweet time. After a week of chemo, my tolerance level is below zero. The thing that wears me out most is people trying to grab my attention or swarming around me like ants. Unfortunately I'm not the only one who's on leave. Sighing heavily, I slowly work my way through the masses. At moments like these my wigs turn into a necessity

I can't live without. But from some people I can't hide. Every woman who has been in the same place I am now immediately recognizes the texture of my fake hair. In the tanning salon, the saleswoman carefully addresses the topic, assuming I'm wearing a wig. Once I confirm, she starts talking to me about her own cancer. She's just been operated on for breast cancer so she knows what she's talking about. She's exactly what you would expect when you think of a woman working in a tanning shop: too blonde, too tanned, her lips too pink. It's a good thing I'm wearing Daisy—she makes the interaction so much easier. I give Miss Fake Tan a kiss on the cheek and take my bottle of bronzer.

On my way to meet Annabel, I hear someone call out "Daisy!" I don't react. They couldn't possibly mean me. But the voice persists. "Daisy! Daisy!" Finally I turn around and see Jan walking out of the crowd "Busted! I knew your Caribbean tan was fake. Maybe I should go there myself one of these days."

"Very funny. Where are you off to?"

"You mean which café? You tell me, you know that old men like me don't lead but follow."

I take him by the arm and together we head to Finch.

It took Annabel some time to get used to my taste in friends. Although Rob's daily wear is jeans and hoodies, Annabel still makes fun of me for hanging out with the elderly. And truthfully, my friend Jan is not far from retiring. She calls me an omni-friend because apparently I'm comfortable around anyone. I can go from arguing philosophy with my classmates in the afternoon to talking fashion with Jan over cocktails. I guess she's right: I never really disliked someone. But now that I have cancer, I'm suddenly allowed to do so. To dislike others, to dislike life. Hate the world. Moan about everything, call everyone names, shoot everything down. Cancer at twenty-one. Life is no longer my friend but my enemy. Pessimism could be my personality and nobody would criticize me. But it's not: even cancer has become my friend.

It has given me my wigs, which grow more and more a part of me. It has given me time and the ability to not waste it, but use it. It has given me Jurriaan; a grocer who carefully inspects each beet, kiwi, and fennel for blemishes before packing them for me; a florist who slips an extra purple orchid into my bag when I'm not looking. Cancer has given me not only ultimate solitude but also ultimate happiness and togetherness. Like my wigs, it's a part of me now.

And now I love everyone even more: nerdy students, trendy urban types, smooth-talking jet-setters, philosophers, and jocks. And goddamn it, because of it, I can't hate my cancer, no matter how hard I try.

Annabel must be right, I really am an omni-friend.

WEDNESDAY, JUNE 1

"Sorry, madam, I'm afraid I can't help you. I really need to see your patient pass."

I repeat my patient number and carefully explain that I have misplaced my pass. Considering the number of times this pass has been put in and taken out of bags, purses, and jeans pockets, it's not surprising that this is already the third time I'm queuing up to have a new one made.

"Miss, starting this Monday we're working with a new system where everything is digitally scanned. Without your pass, I won't be able to do anything for you."

"But that's what I'm here for! A new pass!" The hospital is busy modernizing, but that clearly doesn't mean it's getting more efficient.

"By the way, I can't seem to find you in the system. I mean, you don't look at all like the picture I have here."

"It's a wig."

"Oh, I'm sorry." The girl suddenly changes faces. As if she has said something she shouldn't have.

"Don't worry about it. I quite like her." I tilt Sue a few centimeters from my scalp and bend her back and forth. The girl starts laughing. The laughter does me good but I still feel tense when I call the receptionist.

"Good morning, this is Dr. van der Stap, could you please put me through to Dr. L?"

I'm hiding behind one of the many cement pillars dotting the hospital entrance hall. As doctors are more important than patients, they don't get put on hold for half an hour. I don't have half an hour. I have to be at the radiology department in fifteen minutes. Luckily—and against all expectations—Dr. L can see the fun in this. He of all people is in a position to know that modern hospitals are threatened by bureaucratic inertia.

"Good morning, Dr. van der Stap," Dr. L answers. "Can you stop by my office on your way to radiology?" Behind his uniform, the man actually has quite a good sense of humor.

When I arrive in Dr. L's office, he has a new surprise waiting for me.

"It's a port-a-cath. It's connected by a tube to your heart via your right subclavian vein, underneath your collarbone."

"Aha. In normal-speak, please?"

"It's a small device under your skin that makes it easier to give you IVs."

Unfortunately, the device goes right above my boob. *So much for my summer cleavage.* Still pondering what Dr. L's silicon surprise means for my wardrobe, I leave for the radiology department.

There I'm given a jug of water mixed with radioactive fluid. I have to chug down the whole thing in one hour. There's no doctor or nurse in sight to ask for explanation. An old man—one of those retirees who have found meaning in their life since volunteering at the hospital—tries to do the job.

"You have to finish the whole thing."

"But why?"

"Yes, the whole thing," he repeats.

Sigh. I try one more time. "Are you sure it's for me? Last time they gave me an IV with a different fluid." After all hospitals are just like any other enterprises: things can and do go wrong.

Finally, one of the technicians comes out and explains to me the reasoning behind this change. "Today we'll be scanning the abdomen as well, and in order to see everything properly we have to use a different fluid."

I take a seat. Nothing to do for a whole hour before my scan except wait, imagine terrible things, and chug radioactive fluid. Before I close my eyes I see the same volunteer walking, step by step, to another patient carrying the same jug of water.

THURSDAY, JUNE 2

"Can you imagine? A boob above my boob." Back at Café Finch, I'm trying to explain to Annabel that the trinket to be inserted above my left breast will probably stick out farther than my own modest A-cup. We both burst out laughing. Hers were once compared to watermelons and mine to chickpeas.

"Will there be a cute little tube sticking out of it?" Annabel and I are both finding the whole situation totally hilarious.

"No, thank God, that would be even worse!"

"What do you care anyway, as long as it's going to make you better?"

The giggling fit subsides.

"I guess you're right. I'ts kind of scary though. It makes it all so much more visible and real." I say.

"It is scary. But look at you, you look great. And I'm not talking your latest haircut here."

I smile. It's a sweet thing to say but she can't be right. Since the chemo I have dark circles under my eyes and the lack of any facial hair doesn't help. On the other hand I'm less pale and boney.

"I'm still scared, though. I know my tumors are getting smaller, but what if they can't get rid of them completely?"

"There's no reason to think that."

"No, but it's all I can think about."

Annabel gets up and grabs me tight. "When do you get the results of the scan?"

"Monday."

"Hmm ... And when is your last week in the hospital?"

"If everything goes according to plan ... late July."

"Meaning you can come with us to the South of France then?"

France?! Sun, lavender, fresh markets, smelly cheeses, the sea, and pretty terraces with pretty people reading about even prettier people? "Are you serious?"

"Of course. You always come with us, why wouldn't you this year?"

Yes, why wouldn't I?

FRIDAY, JUNE 3

I'm at the outpatient clinic for some blood tests. Eight patients before me. *Good, a quiet day.* From the recently refurbished coffee shop a little further in the hallway, where everything has been modernized except the old bags behind the counter, I can just keep an eye on the queue. One coffee and two glasses of water later it's my turn. The nurse takes three tubes of blood, stickers them, and stores them away. I only pay attention to three of the numbers: thrombocytes, leukocytes, and red blood cells. Those are the ones that determine whether I need a transfusion.

With my arm taped up, I head to the surgery department, probably the only part of the hospital I haven't been to. Today sucks because it's a long day at the hospital. But it means there will be other days *outside* the hospital, and long days outside the hospital have slowly become my recipe for happiness. I've never been this short on demands. Frankly, it's a great feeling. So I'd rather get it all done in one go. I follow the nurse to meet my newest doctor.

He's definitely a keeper: handsome, youthful face, strong arms, slim waist, no old-fashioned shoes. Let Daisy keep Dr. K, a married family man on brogues.

This doctor starts yet another file. Then he tells me about the operation I'll be having: a cut above my breast, insertion of the "box," and then sewing it all back up. Although it will help spruce up my arms—which now show a trace of death veins and arteries—I don't like the idea of a box sticking out of my skin. It will definitely not make for a nice summer. I can just see myself on the beach with that weird bulge in my chest. Another cancermark. I hope it's the last.

SATURDAY, JUNE 4

It's clothing swap day at my mothers friend Maud's house. Maud never left the seventies. It shows in her clothes, her naughty eyes, and especially in her preference for bangles.

Of all the women, I'm by far the youngest. There are married women with children, divorced women, women with deceased parents, women wearing Spandex, women with Botox, women with sagging tummies and breasts, women with nannies and maids, women with dyed hair. In short: women with a life story.

We drink coffee, eat bonbons, and laugh. I take pleasure in watching all these middle-aged women trying on clothes while enjoying one another's company—and seeing that at fifty-five, they still have the same young girl inside like me.

This thought makes me stop to realize that time is still ticking—ticking on toward a world where it stands still and I could be going much sooner than all these sagging breasts around me. The more I think about it, the further removed I feel from them. It makes me so sad to know time will bring all these stories to an end. Sad that time could take away my weddings and divorces, my children and corrective underwear.

And interest in the purple skirt and gold lamé top I fished out of a pile five minutes earlier is lost. I drop them onto a different pile and am frightened as soon as I see the purple skirt in the hands of a sagging tummy. Without wanting it, I want to want it. I want to care whether I get it for many years to come. But I don't care about the bloody skirt at all.

What I care about is *The Tibetan Book of the Dead*, because even with treatment going well, I'm so scared my illness will always be a part of me. I hate my doctor for having said that the biggest challenge of all is to get rid of it for good. That sentence never leaves my thoughts. Still, it's not something to discuss over drinks in a city café or in a house full of hysterical women, while sipping on a glass of vegetable juice. It's quite lonely making.

I get up to go look for the gold lamé top and find it on my mom's fifty-five-year-old torso.

"What do you think of this top? And this skirt?" she asks.

My mom and Maud are clearly in another state of mind.

"The skirt looks great, but the top isn't working. It's too small for you, more my thing maybe," I lie. My mom gives me a look. A problem with mothers: they always see when you lie. Fathers are much less observant. She hands me over the top. I slip it on.

I want to dance and flirt again. Kiss. Make out. Just like the old days, but now with wig. Off into the unknown of the city night, with an unknown ending. June has arrived, the sun shines longer, and the wind is becoming softer and warmer. Spring fever invades me, from my stomach to my toes. I send a photo in a text message from my phone to the boys with the caption "Emergency" and go in search of a skirt to match the top my mom so kindly handed back to me.

* * *

That night I head to Rain, a new night club in the old casino somewhere in the city center. Inside I'm all butterflies, but on the outside I'm doing my best to look like I own the place. I'm wearing my hottest dress and carry Sue's wild red hair on my head. My eyelashes are all gone now, but my fake lashes for tonight (they only hold three hours) are longer and fuller anyway. My tan from a bottle gives my skin a healthy sheen, which is a good thing because I'm baring a lot of it. As I step into the haze of the club, the light makes the glitter on my dress sparkle. Only the goose bumps on my arms hint at my underlying nerves, but my arm hair has disappeared as well, so no one can tell. It's been only four months that I haven't seen the night, but it feels like new.

The dimness of the nightclub gives me the anonymity I crave. I want to step into the night, to forget everything, to let loose like a girl without a story.

Tonight is dinner with the boys. They are treating me to a night out on the town. We start with dinner; I order codfish in a creamy yellow sauce. The days Jochem does work, he's a trend watcher by profession, one of those guys who is always running and rushing, and who can't sit down for more than five seconds because he'll miss out on the next big thing. I guess being here with him makes me a trendsetter by association. When the second wine bottle is empty, we decide to switch over to mojitos. According to Jan, the rum will certainly kill anything that the chemo missed. I tell him I'll suggest this alternative therapy to my doctor next week.

"Healthy living, Sophie," Dr. L told me. "Eat well, get plenty of sleep, and allow your body lots of rest. It's one big battle in there."

I knock back another gulp of rum. *Ha.* After four months of obedience, the mint and cane sugar taste better than good.

The alcohol slides down my throat without a hint of guilt. Tonight it's food for the soul.

We quickly lose one another when we hit the dance floor. I scan the room and my eyes settle on a swinging tie. I throw my scarlet locks into battle. Sophie would hesitate, but Sue doesn't care. And tonight I'm Sue. I dance along to the rhythm of the music as Sue tickles the nape of my neck.

A few hours later I'm half asleep in a taxi and Tie Boy lies purring with his head on my lap. I'm pleasantly drunk from the mojitos, but also from my night of anonymity. The boy next to me thinks he's met Sue, a trendy girl with a cool haircut. Our conversation hasn't gone beyond house music and sneakers.

"So, what is it you do, actually?" he asks.

"I'm on a gap year."

"Oh. Cool."

He sees nothing of the loneliness I feel, because I've turned my story into a secret. He doesn't know how happy he makes me by running his hands through my hair when we are kissing, not realizing the significance of that movement. How can he know that not only has he won Sue's heart, but also that of Daisy, Stella, Uma, Platina, and Blondie, too?

I watch the city pass by the taxi window. My thoughts are still on the dance floor. Sue who tickled my neck. Tie Boy who was dancing away to the music and told me he liked my style. Jan and Jochem who gave me a wink and told me to go for it.

The taxi pulls up to my house. With a long, passionate kiss I say good-bye to Tie Boy. I get out of the taxi and step back into my own world. The day after tomorrow I'm expected back at the hospital. I tell Tie Boy that I'm going on holiday for a week—heading off to the airport with just a backpack and booking a last-minute flight to Marrakech.

He'll never know that I will visit Marrakech only in my dreams and that I'll be stuck in bed only three streets away. Three streets and a whole world, which, dancing with him, I was able to forget.

At home I take a long look in the mirror. I take off my wig. Put it on again. Off. On. Off. On. I fall asleep, clutching my wig close to me with a smile on my face. Just before I fall asleep I receive a text. It's Jan: "Wigs … A necessity or an opportunity? You naughty girl! Tell me everything tomorrow. Sweet dreams. XJ."

SUNDAY, JUNE 5

I better say it out loud. I've been dreaming of Jur ever since we met. How great a boyfriend he must be! I wish for someone like him in my life, or even someone who is still fighting, like me. Someone who will shuffle in and out of hospitals with me, hold my hand while we do our chemo together, annoy doctors with endless questions, and put his arm around me at night when I wake up crying.

Jur asked me when we first met whether I had a boyfriend.

"No, but lots of great friends," I told him. Now I understand his question. Those friends are there to drink coffee with me, and they loyally visit me in hospital, but then they go back home. To their own beds.

Thanks to Jur, I'm beginning to see my fear of dying from another perspective. Like it's an opportunity, rather than a punishment. He's talking to me about how I can manage my fear. He helps me recognize and name it, cut it up in pieces, and then confront it. He takes my loneliness away, makes me believe I can take on all the cancer in the world. Well ... as long as he sits next to me. The moment he gets up, my newborn spirituality takes off with him. I can't explain what happens inside me when he's with me. I guess I better just call the magic by its name: Jurriaan.

Today, when I arrive at Café Winkel, he's already waiting on the terrace with apple pie and whipped cream. He's wearing a bright green T-shirt that complements his strong tanned arms.

Nice. His dark hair flops over his forehead carelessly. *Even nicer.*

"Hey, new hair color?"

Not only is Jur gorgeous and understanding, he's funny, too. Uma is perched atop my head. These days I prefer Sue's and Uma's bangs to my other wigs because I don't have to bother drawing in eyebrows every other hour or putting on fake eyelashes. *Vive les bangs.* We greet with three kisses on the cheek and dive into speaking our shared language of dactinomycin, dexamethasone, metastases, and other yucky cancer-speak. At one point Jur pauses to look at me. Then he says, "I think I like her best."

The other reason I opted for Uma today: I was hoping my Miss Mia Wallace hairstyle would inject some of her sex appeal.

I feel so clumsy, out of touch, self-conscious. Like a bull in a china shop. I want to give him a self-confident, seductive look and put my lips on his. Even better, I want him to give me that look, that look that makes all the rest disappear, and take me with him into his arms, his life. Why can't I just tell him how I long for him at night? All I do is keep quiet and worry if my wig doesn't live a life on its own. I'm just too afraid that he'll run off if I burden him with the true extent of my feelings.

Cancer-talk it is.

I've brought my file with me, and Jur immediately starts to leaf through it. I'm not sure whether I trust him because he is a survivor or because he is studying medicine, but I do. He thoroughly analyzes all my doctors' decisions. It's nice to hear someone more optimistic than Dr. L, even though Jurriaan doesn't hide from me how lucky I've been.

"Tell me about the port-a-cath" I ask. "My doctor suggested it because I have such trouble getting needled."

"Are you going to get one?" asks Jur.

"Tuesday. Injections are getting harder and harder."

"I had one as well. Look, mine was here." Jur pulls up his T-shirt. A scar from left to right covering the whole width of his hairy chest. I like hairy chests but this freaks me out.

Jur starts laughing. "Not that one, silly. That one was from surgery when they tried to get my tumor out." I sigh, relieved. "It's this one." I can barely see it through his chest hair, but then I see a horizontal scar about eight centimeters long on the left side of his chest.

Great.

I shake my head. "I don't want one."

"You hardly notice it."

"Not if you don't wear tank tops, no."

Jur reassures me, telling me that no one will even notice the difference.

Sure, but I don't have chest hair.

MONDAY, JUNE 6

It's time for the results of my latest scan. Another moment of truth. Sis and I are waiting for Dr. L to call my name. When he appears, I search his greeting for a hint of the results. In his office he looks at me a little longer than usual. His demeanor is getting warmer by the day. I'm even starting to like the guy, who would've thought?

"Well, it's worked. The tumors have decreased yet again. Not quite gone, but ..."

"Did you expect them to be gone this time? Was that the goal?"

"They should be next time. Then we'll have given it all we've got as far as chemo goes. After that it's just maintenance chemo, maybe radiation."

"So the results are good, then?"

"Yes, Sophie, they're good."

I let out the breath I had been holding in. Sis and I softly squeeze each other's hands. Wearing a big smile, I leave the room that once scared the living daylights out of me and I fall into my sister's hug.

Often when I spoke about my falling-out with my sister, friends would say: *That's just sisters.* Not a very satisfying answer for someone who misses her big sister but doesn't have the words to say so, or the courage to let go of her arms. I never understood how we could have started off so close and ended up avoiding each other. Where things went wrong. I just know we tried to live our own lives as far away as possible from each other. If she would start working in a certain café, I would start working in the equivalent of the opposite of that café and vice versa. It's such a gift to drink our tea in the same café again. And the strangest thing is neither of us ever had to apologize. After the news, we just looked at each other and held each other close, never wanting to let go again.

TUESDAY, JUNE 7

I wake up and it takes me a while to realize where I am. I see a lot of white beds and people either sleeping or looking dazed. Then it's all coming back to me: the operating room, the strong arms of the nurse, the deep sleep. But also the mojitos and the dark nightclub and Tie Boy and Jur's chest. I move my right arm and carefully feel my new third breast. I feel a bump with a big bandage around it, just under my collarbone.

Gross.

Unfamiliar nurses rush around. My vision is still fuzzy. Suddenly my grandmother is at my bedside. She must have come in while I dozed off. Oma is very fragile and shy, with big blue eyes. When we're together I always forget that for fifty-six years she led a life without me in it. She has ten of us—grandchildren. Everybody in the family says we look and talk so much like each other. We love spending time together and telling each other stories and jokes.

Oma would never talk pain and misery—I think she thinks it's inappropriate. She lived her worst experiences but best stories in a Japanese camp in Bandung, Indonesia. It's where she was born and brought up, into a Dutch family. When she was fourteen, World War II broke out and they all became prisoners of war. Her father, Louis, was sent to Burma to work on the Burma bridge. She and her mother and sister were sent to war camp. Because there was so little food, the children were always on the lookout for some more. Once she saw a papaya hanging in a tree. It was just hanging there, waiting to be eaten maybe. So she climbed onto the back of her friend, made herself big enough to grasp the papaya, tugged it loose, and then turned around and looked straight into the eyes of a Jap. Eating papayas was a luxury the prisoners of camp were not entitled to. People in camp would call the Japanese "Japs" or "Jappies." She felt her neck hair stand straight up and her muscles stiffen. The man didn't say anything, just looked at her like a statue. She slowly climbed down the back of her friend, put the papaya on the ground in front of the Jap's feet, bowed, and ran off. She never told me what happened the next day when she was called upon. I think she chose to have a selective memory.

She told me this story—and the one of her saving her two white poodles from the Japs—at least a hundred times, and as vividly as Roald Dahl wrote his. She turned them into exciting, naughty and funny bed tales. When she spoke, her big blue eyes were so alive.

When I was still a child, together we did a heck of a lot of retail damage in the city's department store. We would go out grocery shopping, and I always found an excuse to pass by the department store. I found it mesmerizing, this building full of everything. We would re-dress the mannequins, taking their heads off and putting on scarves. It was silly but sweet. And other times we would stay in and bake a cake. We could never get the recipe right. It always came out as a sticky toffee. It turned out that we always put the double amount of butter inside. My granny craves it. Mornings for her are toast with two layers of butter.

The times I ask I ask her a real question, she always takes some time to answer. Once I asked if her years in the war camp were really bad. She was quiet for a while, took another spoon of her soup (she always made soup) and then answered: "Yes, I think they were." I didn't ask further. But now seeing her big blue eyes, I cant help but asking:

"Oma, are you very sad about me?"

She stays quiet for a minute. Her large, piercing eyes tell me she's thinking this over. "Yes," she says.

"Often?"

"Well, the thing is, nothing is any fun anymore."

Silence. I don't know what to say. Not even a joke to pull out of my sleeve. For what feels like minutes we share the silence together, and for as long as those minutes last she seems all I need to be happy. It stings, knowing that she's sad because of me, but it also gives me a warm feeling that we're so closely connected. I get to see her even more often now, and she always brings me something yummy from the organic food store. Today it's nuts, raisins, and plums.

"They're good for you," she says. Carefully, she looks around and asks if my parents or sister have been to visit yet.

"No," I say, suddenly growing restless. All these new faces bustling around are getting to me. I want to go back to my own ward, my own room, and to close my eyes and sleep. "Is it big?" I ask Oma, who has bent over me to inspect the doctor's handiwork. She shakes her head, but her big blue eyes, which have seen so much, can't hide her sadness.

* * *

Later, back in my own ward, Pauke takes off the bandage. The port-a-cath is lodged right below my collarbone. I can't see it and don't dare touch it.

"They've done a very neat job on you," she says while inspecting my bump up close. I smile and wait until everyone has left my room before I take a mirror and look at the horrible bump myself. Two thick pink lines about four inches long run across my collarbone, right over a strange-looking bump. *Two? Why two?* There's nothing neat about them. It's just ugly.

I take out the pictures that Jan took of me flipping off the camera. I always bring them with me to the hospital, for when life's a bitch. This coming Monday I will cross off the twentieth week in my agenda. Then only one more hospital week to go, at the end of July. It doesn't feel like it, but time does go on.

* * *

"Hi, gorgeous, did you sleep well?" My sister's radiant smile flashes as she walks in carrying a basket full of delicious food and birthday banners because it's Mom's birthday today and mine on Saturday. My lethargic neighbors look up.

"Kiss!" I call, sticking out my arms for a hug. I'm always a drama queen when she comes to visit. Sis can never hug me enough and today is no different as she clambers into bed with me. She feeds me pasta—the hospital food is so disgusting you lose just as much weight avoiding it as you do with taking chemo—and takes out some red nail polish to paint my toes.

I tell Sis about my latest fantasy with Dr. K. Sis tells me about her future as an expat wife and her plans to be much more than that. Her darling boyfriend, Kieran, is an English expat—almost as chic as a diplomat, in my book—whose job sends him off to a new location every two years. That's how he and my sister met here, and it's also the reason that Sis and I will be torn apart in six months. He's being posted in Hong Kong, and she's following him in December.

"Two years in a lifetime is nothing," she says.

Two years? Nothing? I love hearing her voice, but not when we're talking years that are like nothing. Or moving across the world. But so much of our lives are lived in the future. All our conversations are built around plans and dreams, and that makes this disease so fucking hard, as I'm not entitled to that vocabulary anymore. I'm an outsider stuck in the present. I don't understand why people say that living in the present brings happiness when it's really the opposite. It sucks. I'm jealous of her life, her future, her beautiful hair, her glowing skin. Her choices. Her freedom. Her health.

We pull the curtain all the way around the bed and talk very softly so as not to disturb the others, but more to not be disturbed. She carefully strokes my bump. I cry. "War wounds," she calls my scars. You can leave symbolism to Sis. While I say "Fuck this fucking cancer," Sis talks about gray skies clearing. We both have our own ways of dealing with it, I guess.

It's comforting to know that she's my guardian angel whenever gray skies are overhead. With her I can let go. There is no such thing as modesty or manners between sisters. When I'm sick and vulnerable, she takes care of me, and when I'm a pain in the ass, she just lets me be a pain in the ass. We're back to being sisters.

Sis selflessly offers up her time to make me vegetable soup and other super-healthy concoctions. When she walks into my room with her homemade pies and pastas, I like to think that I would have done the same for her. But she's always been the caring one. She wanders through the organic food store looking for treats to bring me. Kieran tells me how she struggles with her guilt each time she leaves my bedside and sees my time standing still while her life carries on. I guess it's not less hard to be the person around the sickbed rather than to be the person in it. She has to deal with my illness *and* with the guilt of being the lucky one.

It's another reason why I feel the need to write everything down, if only to fill the gap between us. I don't like gaps or islands. I hate them. I want to be close to Sis, my parents, Oma, my friends, the whole time. I don't want to be separated from them. I don't want to live on an island. I just can't. I really can't.

Dying is not an option.

WEDNESDAY, JUNE 8

It's funny how people assume that, given the choice, I would rather not wear a wig. That when I stick my keys in the front door and hear it fall closed behind me, I'd immediately want to rid my head of all that fakeness, toss my wig on the floor, and sigh with relief.

It's not like that at all. Often I forget I have anything on my head that shouldn't be there. I've gotten so used to my wigs that they are set up on my dresser as if they have always been there. They're just a part of me now.

Underneath my clothes and wigs I'm starting to look more and more like a cancer patient. Not only do I have the bald scalp, but now I have the scarred body to match. I'm fascinated by this thing sticking out above my breast, connecting me to my IV pole. I can't stop touching it. It moves around awkwardly, like a Ping-Pong ball under my skin.

I always associated cancer with old people and unhealthy lifestyles, but the past few years have shown me that nothing could be further from the truth. Even my beautiful mom and Angelina Jolie got to deal with it.

People assume that cancer comes with spirituality. I'm not afraid of a little spirituality. But it's quite another thing to go and sit on a cushion and hide myself behind a wall of Buddhism. To say whatever happens is fine because I live in the present. Blagh. Although I've always felt attracted to Buddhism, I can't see what to make of it now. It's all about acceptance and letting go. But to me, accepting being a cancer patient is like giving up my defenses. I have not accepted being one and something tells me I shouldn't. That the day I do accept being bedridden 24/7, walking around bald and ugly or becoming a person who doesn't care about her fantastic pair of new shoes anymore, is like closing a pact with death.

There are people who ask me whether I have changed. It sounds like a simple question to answer, but how am I supposed to know really? I still hang out with my friends. I still spend unhappy hours in the cramped fitting rooms at Zara. I still read my books, watch lame television, and flip through *Vogue*. These activities are still part of me. Some people's eyes tell me they shouldn't, that magazines are not bringing me anything, that the way I look is not important on the verge of dying. Well, to me it is. What some people call unimportant really isn't at all. When I transform myself into a femme fatale, I feel like one. When I do my makeup and put on high heels and a wig, I feel stronger, bigger, and less afraid. My wigs don't only make me anonymous; they give me a chance on another, parallel life where cancer doesn't exist.

FRIDAY, JUNE 10

"Joining us for dinner tonight? We're ordering takeout." Nurse Esther pops her head around the curtain. She's come to rescue me from the shared room. I'm fed up with the sour faces of my neighbors, and a single room became available down the hall. Good news for me, but not for the family of the empty bed. An ugly thought comes to mind: "One person's dead is someone else's bread."

Esther isn't like the other nurses. All the nurses are nice, but Esther is nice *and* beautiful, and most important, young. I can talk to Esther about everything I'm interested in outside the hospital. Things like favorite nightspots, music and romances. Her life is more than just working in a hospital. She usually only works on Tuesdays and Wednesdays, but this week she's working Friday as well. On the weekends she spins in clubs all around Amsterdam, her wild hair blazing in the spotlights. Just like me, she watches *Desperate Housewives* on Tuesday evenings, which means we can enjoy our shared TV passion together. I wish that all the other hospital residents were fans of the show too. Maybe then they would stop ringing for the nurses and interrupting the sound on the telly when it's on. Unfortunately, it's always rush hour during the show, and Esther has to run around juggling chemo bags.

Esther takes a seat on my bed. She tells me about last weekend's party at Paradiso; I tell her about dancing and kissing Tie Boy.

"Got a picture?"

"No."

"Shame. Which wig were you wearing?"

"Sue. He didn't notice a thing."

"You think you're going to see him again?"

"No. Can't have him asking me too many questions."

"Why not?"

"Who wants to date a girl with cancer?"

"Sophie, you shouldn't think like that."

"Besides, I might feel more like Uma or Daisy when I see him, and then what do I tell him?"

Esther gives me a smile. "So are you having dinner or not?"

"Yes, I'd love to. Are you ordering now?"

"No, not until five." She puts down the menu on my bed and unplugs me from the wall socket. In hospitals people eat at six P.M. In the end we are in a home for the elderly.

We're off to room 2. Nurse Betty is taking care of the rest of the move, bringing my slippers and books and other things. It's a quarter to four, a strange time of day in the hospital. Esther has only just started her shift, but I already have the longest part of my day behind me. Most of my visitors come in the evenings. Tonight my parents and Oma are coming, and then Annabel and Rob. Until then it's just me, my IV pole, and the clock tower through the window. Until then I'll be on my island. As I don't like being on my island, I don't write about it. Nothing happens here anyway, except for drowning in dreadful thoughts.

* * *

"So tell me about this boy." Rob sits next to my bed, his legs stretched. It's after dinner time, but the evening still has to start.

"He wore a tie, cool sneakers, and he was a good kisser."

"And?"

"And that's it. I told you, that's as far as I go. He didn't even know I was wearing a wig."

Rob laughs.

"He kept running his hands through my hair while he was kissing me. I can't believe he didn't notice anything."

Rob laughs even louder and grabs ahold of me. He likes to squeeze people, so much so that he'll squeeze the air out of you if you aren't careful.

"What are you up to this weekend?" I ask.

"I'll pop by Finch later, I think. To celebrate your birthday at midnight."

"That's sweet. I'm allowed out tomorrow. I'll probably feel awful, but I'd like to see you all."

"Doll, of course we'll stop by, with flowers and all for the birthday girl. A ridiculously huge bunch."

Rob leaves and I hear his cowboy boots stomping off down the empty corridor.

I can see Esther running around through my door. Energetic and caring Esther—so vibrant next to the white and sterile surroundings. I look up and see that the bag of yellow chemo fluid is almost empty. In a few minutes' time my IV will start beeping and Esther will come in to refresh my supply. And when she comes, I'll be at my baldest. No wig, no smile, no cover-up to pretend I'm doing just fine.

"My friend Jochem is coming in the morning. Remember, I told you about him? You have to meet him," I tell Esther when she comes in.

"Oh, why?"

"Well, he just called and said that he once hooked up with you. I told him no way. He's always making up wild stories."

"I don't think I've ever hooked up with a Jochem," Esther says, laughing.

"Well, we'll see about that tomorrow."

* * *

We accidentally run into each other in an unfamiliar city. He's on a business trip; I'm on the prowl. A combination of unexpected circumstances has brought me to the lobby of his hotel. It's one of those hotels where you could stay for months without ever longing for your own soap, bathrobe, or toothbrush. He's sitting in the lobby with a group of other gray suits, at the bar. Probably here for a conference. They're drinking, smoking cigars, and laughing with whiskey on their breath. They're relaxed, aware of their temporary escape, looking for adventure.

I walk into the hotel in search of the address of a dinner party that I haven't been able to find for the past ten blocks. I can feel my toes burning after barely an hour in my new heels, and my tight skirt is creeping up to great heights. I feel the attention of the group of men at the bar shift in my direction. I carefully and seductively return their gaze. *His* gaze. Sitting right there amid the men is Dr. K.

Heading toward him, I slow my step, bend my head, and toss back my long brown hair. For some men I feel pure lust. Dr. K is one of them. Uma is just perfect for expressing that desire. I smile, aware of all my feminine wiles, as I walk toward him. Foreplay is unnecessary. This one's in the bag.

We escape upstairs to his room. Playfully, but with the utmost concentration, he unbuttons my blouse without ever losing my gaze, uncovering my black lace bra. One hand moves toward my breast while the other unhooks my bra. My nipples harden between his fingers. He kisses them, kisses my neck, kisses me. Faster and more intensely now. He picks me up and carefully lays me down in the middle of the bed. We disappear beneath his sheets and stay there all night, until we fall asleep exhausted, curled up and twisted around each other. We don't wake up until the afternoon noises of the unfamiliar city come closer.

Five days in the hospital, five days to let my mind wander. Five mornings, afternoons, and evenings in which we enjoy each other's company in the seductive anonymity of a hotel. I fantasize about breakfast, visiting museums, and lengthy dinners. But especially about night, when nothing exists beyond us and his sheets.

A good thing that my tumors didn't reach my dreams.

SATURDAY, JUNE 11

In front of me are twenty-two yellow roses! I don't like yellow roses, but I'm still grinning from ear to ear as I count them. Twenty-two exactly. With a card: *Sorry I couldn't bring them myself*. No name, but there's no need. I know who they're from. I have only one friend who would buy me yellow roses: Jan. We talk matching colors as much as matching boyfriends; he's the only one who knows how much I dislike the color yellow.

Birthdays are much more fun when you're sick and you realize you're still around to grow another year older than they are when you're healthy and you have to think about how you're aging. The nurses come into my room singing "Happy Birthday," with Pauke leading the pack. She doesn't waste any time adjusting my IV.

I don't like to waste time either and have already packed my things. Nurse Betty was on night duty last night and he made sure my pump worked a little faster than usual, so my chemo bag is already empty. Luckily, my blood count is on the high side today, so I can skip the blood transfusion.

There's a wheelchair waiting for me today. *Must be a birthday privilege*. I try to protest the wheelchair, but when I attempt to get up, a mix of colors and dots swim before my eyes. I roll from the ward to the elevator. Blagh. Just twenty-two and in a wheelchair.

MONDAY, JUNE 13

"I think I scared off Tie Boy yesterday."

"Did you see him?"

"Yeah, yesterday, on the terrace at Café Winkel. He didn't recognize me at first. I was wearing Blondie."

"What did you tell him?"

"Experimental hairdresser. He either thinks I'm really trendy or completely insane. Anyway, it'll be the last time. I didn't feel like talking about my illness, and I'm not enough of an actress to continue seeing him."

"Come here." Rob plants a kiss on my forehead and envelops me in a bear hug so tight it hurts a little.

"Sweetie?" he says.

"Yes?" I look up at him, wondering what the suddenly serious tone in his voice means, but he's just smiling at me.

"Never mind."

TUESDAY, JUNE 14

Platina is made to impress, and that's exactly what I feel like doing when I'm wearing her. I don't just enjoy the freedom that comes with anonymity, but also the freedom that comes with saying: *Yes indeed, I'm wearing a wig*. She's so confident and so careless about what other people think that I can only follow her: there's no room for doubts and self-consciousness. There's only room for amplifying, adding, exaggerating. Hence I choose my green feather eyelashes that enlarge my own by three times the size, a smooth black eyeliner and a dramatic evening dress to top things off. If I let chemo rule my world I would be upside down in bed right now. At this point there's only a few good blood cells left in my body. Therefore I happily let Platina decide. I can't fool my body for a whole night, but for a quick visit into nightlife it will do.

Now all I need is Annabel. She's dining in a new restaurant in town and sends her boyfriend, Bart, to pick me up. I gratefully accept. The plan is to use the few happy blood cells that are still swimming around in my body for some fun, not for the road.

In the restaurant all eyes are on me. With Platina it's never sure if it's for wearing a wig (nobody can overlook that fact) or for wearing a wig that actually looks good on me.

"There's my girl, not missing out on a single opportunity to be noticed. You look great. Hope you're hungry, we ordered for masses."

I look at the food, which looks delicious, but I'm not feeling hungry at all.

"Some wine?"

"Nah, I better have some juice."

"So with whom do we have the pleasure of dining tonight?" Bart's friend asks.

"Platina."

"Well, you know what they say, it's all in a name. I assume Platina has expensive taste?"

"She can have, indeed."

"Does she like dancing?"

"She loves dancing."

"So you will join us then. There's a new club opening tonight."

"Unfortunately not tonight."

Annabel takes over the conversation. "You have to try this, just take a little bite. It's too good."

"How are the cocktails?"

"I'm not going to lie. They're the best in town."

"Haha bitch. Surely not as good as the juice."

"Surely."

WEDNESDAY, JUNE 15

I'm in the back of the line at the organic food store on Westerstraat, armed with a recycled carrier bag. I refuse to go on a special cancer diet; there are too many to choose from and they all say something different. I do, however, believe in vitamins, antioxidants, and organic produce.

My basket is filled with beets, quinoa, pumpkin seeds, and goat's milk. I'm still a beginner to this healthy-lifestyle thing. This morning I surprised myself when I managed to squeeze an entire fennel bulb through the juicer. I've always thought of myself as a reasonably healthy girl, avoiding junk food and too much booze and all that, but in front of these trays of millet, buckwheat and quinoa I'm quite the amateur. How does one pronounce quinoa?

I inspect the contents of another customer's basket as they are being scanned: seaweed, algae, and some packages I can't identify. Behind the counter is an array of tablets and bottles: spirulina, chlorella, aloe vera, ginseng, and a lot of other mystery. I listen to the conversation between the other customer—who obviously speaks fluent health guru—and the girl behind the counter, wearing Birkenstocks. You have to be careful with people wearing Birkenstocks outside the hospital. Before you know it they'll try to convert you to their entire lifestyle.

A few jars disappear into her hemp bag. I sigh and decide to leave the Chinese herbs for the time being.

On my way home I pick up a class schedule from one of the many yoga studios in the neighborhood. “Yoga”: such a promising word. During each class I diligently try to stretch and bend my stiff body parts into increasingly difficult positions. That’s all there is to it, really: stretching, stretching, and more stretching, from your legs and arms to your toes and fingers.

After yoga is meditation. *Pfft, meditation, what a mission.* It’s way harder than it looks, especially when you forget what you’re doing it for. To be honest, I’ve never really gotten it—not in meditation class (which seems like an oxymoron to me), or when I was surrounded by it in Tibet and India. I’m still trying to master the contemplation and concentration phase and hoping I’ll stumble into meditation.

What a cliché I’ve become: getting sick, contemplating spirituality, trying to get healthy by squeezing fennel bulbs and broccoli stems. Seducing men wherever I go, to forget my loneliness. Truthfully, I’d rather have a boyfriend on the couch than all the rest of it. Then at least being flexible and lighting candles in the evening would serve some purpose.

FRIDAY, JUNE 24

"And that's why I need to have an MRI of my brain," I tell him.

Dr. L sighs and says something like: "If it will make you feel better, but I'm not concerned." He picks up the phone to make an appointment.

I've convinced myself there's something growing in my brain. Something like a brain tumor. I've been suffering from constant headaches for a few weeks now. I feel stabbing pains and hear helicopters landing between my ears, and my nose is running like crazy. In the medical library I read that a runny nose can be an indicator of something wrong in your head. And there have been cases of my disease in which brain tumors have led to rhabdomyosarcomas like mine. After a few helicopter rides/panic attacks and afternoons researching in the medical library, I've presented my haphazard argument to Dr. L.

Dr. L hangs up the phone. "Wednesday, June twenty-ninth, at seven fifty A.M.," he says. "Did you write that down?"

"Yes, this coming Wednesday at seven fifty."

"Good, then I'll see you afterward for your day treatment."

"Fine. How many chemos are we at now?"

"That's nine, ten, eleven—wait a minute, twelve—yes, the twelfth. Goes by fast, doesn't it? Almost halfway." Dr. L looks at me encouragingly.

"When will I get the results of the MRI?"

"As soon as possible. I hope the day after. Then I can tell you more about the rest of your treatment. I'm going to a team meeting in which we'll discuss the possibilities of radiation and operating. But as I said before, an operation, in my opinion, is not an option."

So, Dr. L is gossiping with his friends about my treatment plan. If they want to cut me open, now is the time. Every doctor I've confronted with my file shakes their head no, but I keep hoping for an operation. Better to have three treatments to cure me than two. Maybe my luck will turn. My tumors could look completely different after six months of chemotherapy.

"Oh, and this wig"—he nods at Platina—"does nothing for you. It makes you look old."

I sigh. "I feel old."

WEDNESDAY, JUNE 29

I am one big ball of nervous energy. For the past twenty minutes I've been lying with headphones on and a mask over my face, listening to a sound like a jackhammer.

The ruckus suddenly stops. Two faces appear above me. "We need to inject some extra contrast fluid for a better image."

Shit, that means they see something. There's something there. Shit, it's in my head.

"Is it bad?" I ask.

The two unfamiliar heads look at each other and call over the radiologist. I'm freaking out. If they won't give me an answer, it must be bad.

The radiologist looks down at me. "Everything looks normal so far, but we can't confirm anything until Dr. L has taken a look. We're just going to take one more image."

I burst into tears of relief as the sound of the cement drill starts up again.

Relieved to be out of there, I arrive at the day-treatment outpatient clinic. Pauke is rushing around. "Cyclone Pauke," as her colleagues call her. I say hello to everyone, take a seat near the window, and stick a cookie in my mouth as I press PLAY on my iPod. *Bring on the chemo.*

THURSDAY, JUNE 30

Rob and I sit on the waterfront in a small town on the Amstel river. We drink, eat, and talk, but mostly we are waiting for a phone call. When I look down at my plate, I see that I've hardly touched my food. I've been listlessly pushing my salad around on my plate for the past twenty minutes. Rob, as usual, is eating something red and meaty; I, as usual these days, am eating something green and healthy.

My phone rings. My fork misses my plate and I stick it into some meaty substance on Rob's.

It's Dr. L.

"I've spoken with my colleagues and everyone agrees that an operation is not an option. We're moving straight on to radiation."

"Oh."

"It's still too dangerous to operate that close to your lungs. We'll cause more damage than good."

"So, what now?"

"I've made an appointment for you next week with the radiologist. He'll explain everything."

"What about my MRI?" I ask.

"The MRI looked good, exactly like they told you. There's nothing in your brain."

Deep sigh. It took a paranoia-induced MRI to realize I trust Dr. L more and more.

"No other complaints?"

"No."

"Are you feeling okay?"

"Yes, just a bit more washed out than usual."

"That's probably due to your low blood count. Perhaps we should get you another blood transfusion. When is your next blood test?"

"Monday."

"All right. Stop by my office and see me then. Have a good weekend."

I don't know if I'm relieved or scared. I wouldn't have been too happy about hard-core surgery and a twenty-centimeter-long scar like Jur's stretching across my stomach, but losing one of my three treatment options doesn't feel great either. Jur explained to me that even though chemo kills a lot of the cancer, a local treatment such as surgery or radiation is necessary to get rid of every last cell. Now I understand what my doctor meant when he said that it's even more of a challenge to keep my illness at bay once we get rid of the tumors. The toughest part is hunting down the very last cancer cells in my body.

Rob's arm finds its way around me. And there it is, in between the arm squeezes, hugs, and friendly kisses: a long look, followed by a long kiss. Rob kisses away my fear.

It must be a combination of the way he looks at me, his firm hugs, and—let's not forget—the vintage Jaguar that made the butterflies in my stomach fly around in a frenzy.

"Rob?"

"What is it?"

"I've got butterflies."

"Butterflies?"

"Yes, you give me butterflies. These past few days."

"Oh, dear." Rob always calls me "hon," "cutie," or "sweetie." He gives me another kiss and squeezes my leg. Rob always likes to grab me—arm, leg, or butt.

"Come on, let's go, cutie." He gets up, pays the bill, and takes me by the hand. "*The Sopranos* at my place?"

"Yes."

"Do you want to stay over?"

"Yes."

"You know I'm far too old for you."

"Twice as old, to be exact." We laugh.

"This isn't right. You can stay over and we'll sleep, that's it."

FRIDAY, JULY 1

I open my eyes. Someone is lying next to me in bed. I blink, and for a minute he's gone. Open, closed, open, closed.

Open.

Deeply tanned shoulders, back, and arms. Brown hair speckled with gray, and that oh-so-handsome face. He looks as if he just stepped out of a Marlboro campaign. He has his arms crossed and his eyes closed. I sigh with relief; he hasn't seen me naked—wigless, that is. Without making a sound I turn and hunt around for Uma, who must have fallen off while I was sleeping and turning. I touch my scalp, which has stretched—without any trace of my hairline and eyebrows—into the shape of an egg: my face has lost not only its features but also its humanity.

I sit up straight in bed. It's still dark outside. Carefully, I slide Uma onto my head, seeking some comfort beneath her soft, dark strands. I crawl back under the sheets, close against Rob's warm body. Last night I made love and fell asleep as Uma. This morning I woke up as myself, not capable of anything I did last night. Careful not to lose my wig, I give him a kiss on his nose.

His eyes slowly open. A smile. "Hey, gorgeous. Did you sleep well?"

I nod.

"What's the time?"

I shrug.

We stare at each other and stare some more. Strange how a face changes when you get closer. We both smile but can't take our eyes off each other. His hand strokes my arm. I snuggle up closer. And then we kiss. Beneath the sheets our legs find one another. I feel my wig gliding over my head and fear takes over. Does he notice? Am I repellant? I carefully try to get my wig back in shape. I want to feel feminine. Sexy, desirable, irresistible. But I feel everything but. Maybe this is why I fear my scalp so much: being pretty and attractive is apparently not so much about seducing men as it is about seducing life. Representing death, it's like life is slipping away from me. The life that was always there. All I had to do was get up and smile. Now every time I put on a wig, it's like I'm picking up the pieces she left for me.

"Sweetie, why don't you just take it off?"

"No."

"You're beautiful without it."

"I can't."

Rob remembers me from my days of messy buns, political ambitions, and wine drinking on the terraces of Amsterdam. But he also recognizes me as a lost little girl who doesn't know where to turn.

"Rob, I'm so scared sometimes."

"Oh, honey, of course you're scared. I'm scared too. But they're going to make you better. I'm sure of that."

"How do you know that for sure?"

"They're doctors. It's their job."

* * *

Snuggling and *The Sopranos* turned into passion and sex. Therefore I keep two of my wigs at my bed table. I can't make love without.

"Honey, are you coming?" Rob has gotten up; the bath is full. We stay in for ages, until our fingers shrivel up and the warm water cools off. Then back to bed. Tomorrow I'll pass by my wig store to get some tape.

SATURDAY, JULY 2

The summer sales are on, and after a morning of shopping, I met up with Jochem for some lunch. He polishes off his beer and orders another. I want to head back to the shops, but Jochem's just settling in.

As I listen to Jochem's story with one ear, I inspect my new purchases. Behind him, a man in a suit is passing by. A well-cut suit. I pay less and less attention to Jochem's story and peek over his shoulder as the suit walks by. Is he a lawyer? A consultant? In IT? Married? On a business trip? Kids? A mistress? Daisy's type?

I cross my legs and wiggle my foot up and down. I look at the high heels peeking out from under my jeans and smooth my hair. I take a sip from my sparkling water and leave a set of glossy lip prints on the edge of my glass. My lips are my biggest asset. Full, thick lips. Perfect for a flirt like me.

I was fourteen when I met my first love. His name was Emiliano, and he was the paperboy on our street. I gave up my teen heartthrobs for him in a heartbeat. Even Steven Tyler and Mick Jagger were no match. Young and naive, I didn't think I would ever be parted from Emiliano and his Vespa. It didn't occur to me that there might be more Vespas zooming around town. Those evenings spent on the back of his white scooter awakened my desires, and a new world opened up to me. It was cheap-romance-novel stuff, but I thought we would be together forever.

"Which name can I put the tab on?" the waitress asks. I look up in surprise, without pulling my head out of the clouds.

"Daisy."

Jochem smiles and then chatters on uninterrupted. About his acting career, the waitress's backside, and his belly—a very cute but not-so-sexy belly. Problematic because Jochem likes to wear trendy, tight T-shirts. He says that his belly only shows up when he drinks beer. Unfortunately, that's pretty much every day, sporadically substituted for health shakes. That's why I call him "Bunny" instead of "Honey."

Jochem is a model on the side. With his stomach held in, he regularly attends castings that land him jobs in front of a camera, washing his hair with L'Oréal or cooking Bertolli pasta with very happy girls in a kitchen. With his handsome face, heavenly blue eyes, and endless charm, he always manages to talk his way out of parking tickets and other annoying situations. He's a dreamer like me, but sometimes he finds it difficult to separate his dreams from his parking tickets. For Jochem, Amsterdam is like his own little Hollywood, where vain dreams become reality. Starstruck by a few modeling jobs and some luck at the casino, he has a hard time with regular things like taking out the trash, making his own sandwiches, or having an office job. Great for me because he always has time to go shopping with Daisy.

We stroll back alongside the shop windows. The grumpy faces of the bored saleswomen stare straight through me. *Boredom—now that's something I haven't felt for a long time.*

TUESDAY, JULY 5

Talking to doctors has its complications. Until six months ago, I had a completely different idea of how hospitals worked. I saw sick people coming in through the entrance and leaving again through the exit, healed. Now I see blood samples getting lost, IV needles missing the vein three times in a row, files going missing, and multiple doctors prescribing something different for the same ailment. And it's as if they're speaking in tongues. Forget French, I need to take lessons in Doctor-Speak 101.

Dr. L tells me, "Your right lung is responding well, and the pleural soft-tissue mass on the right side of the thorax has decreased. There was an issue with the nodular pleural structures, but rib six posterior shows figuration of the bone. Soft-tissue mass two in the lining of the lateral abdomen has also decreased. There is still a right anterobasal horizontal-shaped disfiguration in the lung." I take a copy of the file with me and plug the information into my computer. My spell-check freaks out.

* * *

Today Dad and I have come to a different hospital, outside of Amsterdam, to discuss my chances for radiation. Now that radiation is on the agenda, it has taken over the royal seat of chemo. Suddenly it's the radiation treatment that's going to make the difference, not the chemo. Chemo was just a warm-up, new doctors say. While my father closely inspects the coffee vending machine, I watch every movement of the nurse behind the reception desk.

A door opens and a doctor appears. He's wearing glasses and has hair that falls wildly over his ears. He calls out a name and a geriatric man in front of me gets up. His wife shuffles after him.

Another door opens and a younger doctor appears. I think midthirties. *Will he be my radiologist?* He walks to the reception desk and leaves the file he has in his hands. Then he walks back into his office without calling out any name.

"Van der Stap?"

I turn around. I get up and offer the third candidate my hand. He looks at me very briefly as if to underline that I'm just another patient. So this is my radiotherapist: Dr. O.

He sketches my lungs and draws two big arrows where the radiation will be aimed. He weighs me and examines my glands. The scale shows fifty-five kilos. That's one less kilo than last month.

His thoughts on my case are inconclusive, and therefore not very encouraging. "A number of things are still unclear to me. It won't be straightforward, that we know for certain. I'll be in touch with my colleagues in Rotterdam and Utrecht before I come to a conclusion. I want to hear what they think of your condition. Dr. N in Rotterdam is renowned."

I leave the office, feeling anything but reassured. *Why can't they stand to be a bit more cheerful?* On our way home I tell Dad that I feel glad being under Dr. L's care. That he's actually a very nice man.

Dear Jan pops by to say hello just as I am coming back from the hospital. He brought along the sweetest chocolates. "Have some, we can't have you too healthy. That's dangerous."

I give him a kiss and a hug. "I want to go out. Do you feel like trying on some wigs?"

"Wigs? Yes, baby, let's go. I can use one too. But first serve this old man some tea and chocolates."

I spin in circles in a now-familiar chair. Jan happily wanders up and down the aisles and comes back wearing the most hideous wigs, making a complete fool out of himself, but he eventually brings back a sophisticated blonde as well.

"Jan, hand it over. I'm sure she looks better on me."

"I wouldn't be so sure of that."

Well, she does. So much for modesty. Meet Pam. Pam, the girl next door. Pam, Jennifer Aniston's younger sister. Look-how-my-hair-blows-naturally-in-the-wind Pam. And the best part: she doesn't even look like a wig. Pam is the hair I always wished for: pretty without looking pretentious. I take another look in the mirror. I'm beginning to recognize the face that I see there. It makes me wonder if maybe I could actually be like Pam.

We stroll back together and it's nice, *really* nice, strolling with these beautiful blonde streaks that blow in the soft wind and with my dear friend over the quiet, sunny canals. We talk, we laugh, we say nothing. This is the part of cancer that leaves me clueless: I never felt as happy in my life as I have at certain moments in the last couple of months, strolling with Jan through town, getting together around the kitchen table with my family, gluing myself into my sisters arms.

People say without our health we have nothing. I don't have my health, but I have Jan and Rob and Annabel and my family. If I had to choose, the choice would be easy.

I can't wait to see Rob's face. Today is the seventh time I can surprise him with a new look.

* * *

The day I found out I had cancer, I no longer had to play by the rules. I can do, say, and think whatever I like. Everyone pities me, everyone wants to lend a helping hand. I sometimes worry that this will make me forget what life is really like. I can get away with anything; the truth is that cancer just makes me more loved. Every time I turn up in a new wig, I hear, "Oh, wow, this one looks great as well. It's just amazing the way you're handling this." Apparently cancer impresses people. People think they admire me for how well I handle it, but they don't get that I'm not "handling" anything, I'm just going through it.

My wigs help me hide what I want to hide and to emphasize what I want to show off. The wig I choose to put on my head creates the space I need for the mood I'm in. The cancer is always there. When I fall asleep, wake up, do the grocery shopping. But when I put on a wig, I am there as well. It's as if I'm taking its part on stage. Wearing my illness on the outside makes the situation easier for others and for me. It can be hard to understand other people's problems, and that's where my wigs come in: I can't think of a better way to show my vulnerability, and myself, than by wearing a different wig every day.

Now my wigs make it easy to switch worlds. As Uma, my taste in men draws me to crumpled T-shirts pulled out from the bottom of the laundry basket and worn with a five-o'clock shadow. But I also love neatly ironed Armani suits and matching loafers, accessorized with a dazzling white smile—that's Platina's style. As Blondie, I love a rough-and-tumble Marlboro Man; smooth-talking jet-setters are perfect for Stella. Sue is all about the philosopher exhaling his big ideas with the smoke from his joint. And the jock with a heart of gold but no ideas at all? A perfect match for Daisy. My wigs are becoming more and more of a solution, rather than a problem.

WEDNESDAY, JULY 6

The urge to put down my words on paper keeps on chasing me. It wakes me up at night, it pulls me away from underneath the warm blankets early in the morning, and it makes me a very bad listener: I'm constantly drifting away in new words waiting to be seized on paper. It helps me understand the incomprehensible, but that's not why the words won't stop. Truthfully, I'm scared shitless to cease to exist. To leave life behind and everybody in it.

We sit at a corner table in Rob's favorite Italian restaurant. On my way to the bathroom I walk by the kitchen, where delicious food smells fill me with warmth as I pass. In the bathroom, I touch up my fake eyebrows in the mirror and comb Platina. When I walk back, Rob is talking to the owner, Salvatore. They hug tightly. On the table there are two yellow Livestrong bracelets.

"For you," Salvatore says. "Rob told me about your illness. I'm sure you're going to make it. Our son, Marco, didn't. He passed away last year. Leukemia."

I swallow a big lump that has suddenly found its way to my throat. Salvatore looks me intensely in the eyes. He is wearing the bracelet himself. For a brief moment, his pain is my pain and my pain is his pain as we sit drinking wine together. When he's gone, Rob and I slip on the bracelets. I want to be connected to him via a bond that's impossible to break.

A few hours later, I surf my new friend Lance's website and buy one hundred yellow bracelets. Indirectly, I owe him a lot, too much to count. One hundred yellow dollars, to make the lives of all those other baldies a little better. It might be a bit much, but ten bracelets look so silly beside the recommended one hundred and optional thousand. I click CONFIRM, happy to contribute to my own destiny.

I go to bed and snuggle up close to Rob. I'm feeling scared but keep it to myself. I don't know what to say, anyway. And it always ends in a simple "Everything is going to be fine."

How many times did Marco have to listen to that crap?

THURSDAY, JULY 21

Before the radiation starts, it's vacation time. Fourteen days of sunshine, good food, French wine, bikinis, sandals, and not a white coat to be seen. Two weeks of pure bliss in the South of France with Annabel!

When I was five years old, there was one stuffed animal in the mall that I wanted more than anything, and I threw a temper tantrum until I got her. Her name is Minoe, and she's a little plush kitty. Minoe has loyally shared my bed for the past sixteen years, which is much more than I can say for my boyfriends. She's been everywhere I've been, but I think her favorite trip was to the Himalayas.

There she found herself in between the ducks and the yaks, the Chinese and the Tibetans. At first, Minoe wasn't sure what to make of all those green expanses, bright turquoise lakes, icy blue skies, and sparkling mountaintops. It was chilly for a cat that had never left modern, bustling Amsterdam. By now, Minoe is well traveled and experienced in swapping her spot in my bed for a tent in Iran, a sleeping bag in Nepal, a houseboat in Kashmir, or a sheepskin rug in Rajasthan.

And soon we'll be heading out into the big, wide world again. "Five more nights," she softly purrs in the ears of the nurses. Five more nights before she's back in that world.

SATURDAY, JULY 23

I've been released from the hospital! *Indefinitely released.* My coveted discharge document is beside me. I look at it as I lie in bed. My last night in the hospital has been slept, my last morning has dawned. The last bag of IV fluid dangles from the arms of my tall guardian. I've spent thirty-five nights here. The first six months—twenty-seven weeks—have passed. I look at my IV with mixed feelings. He's silent.

No more sleepovers on C6, no more hospital smell or chemo pee. *Never again?* I don't dare say it out loud just yet. From now on it's just maintenance chemo as an outpatient and radiation at the hospital in Rotterdam.

Farewell, C6. Rotterdam, here we come. *Will Bas miss me? Does he miss the others who came before me? How many of us does he miss? How many of us have walked these corridors?* I peek through an open door, on the lookout for another me hiding under a wig, but all I see are old people picking up the last fragments of their lifes.

My father has come to pick me up. He gives me a hand putting my clothes and books in my bag. I had packed most of it yesterday afternoon, eager to get out of here. I'm happy to see him. When my mother is worried it shows immediately on her face, but my father either knows very well how to hide his, or he really has only one credo: carpe diem.

"Good morning, princess, did you enjoy your last week in paradise?" Dad doesn't speak easily about things that matter.

My father is the type of man who hangs around the kitchen on the lookout for someone to laugh with. He communicates through his humor. I guess he gets so uncomfortable when it comes to difficult situations that he always has a joke up his sleeve to make things appear less grave. I guess I'm my father's daughter in many ways.

The moment he walks into my room and into my life with his big grin, the hospital feels like just a little bump to deal with. There are more important things in life: the family dinner tonight and laughter, to start with.

Mom doesn't always understand his humor, or mine for that matter since I inherited his. The other day I felt a small lump on my lip that resulted in a joke with Dad about a lip tumor. Dad and I had a huge laugh about it while Mom was looking at us like we belonged to somebody else's family.

The elevator opens in the garage under the hospital. The odor is as bad as on my ward. When my father turns on the motor, a CD starts playing automatically: the Rolling Stones. During the journey home we don't say a word to each other but both shout along with the lyrics, turning the volume up more and more.

MONDAY, JULY 25

One more hospital visit before scooting off—this time in Rotterdam, where Dr. N, my new radiologist, practices. The radiologists are ready and waiting for me, armed with their protractors, tracers, and other measuring equipment. Dr. N is like a gift from the gods compared to the other doctors I've encountered in the past six months. He looks like Professor Calculus from *Tintin* and isn't afraid of an encouraging shoulder pat. I warm to him immediately.

Feeling hesitant, I take a seat opposite him. Dr. O in Amsterdam didn't exactly fill me with hope. I'm happy he passed me on to Dr. N.

"I've looked at your photos, and I have to say, this won't be an easy task."

"Oh."

"The tumors are located in an area that is hard to reach, meaning we won't be able to radiate as strongly as we would like."

"Oh."

"There's not much I can say at this point, but I don't want to discourage you. I've cured cases of juvenile cancer similar to yours."

"Right." My hands start to itch and sweat.

Dr. N continues. "Before you go, we'll take some X-rays so that I can start calculating your dose straightaway. After that, we'll make a mold of your chest that will be turned into a mask for you to wear during the treatment. That way we don't have to mark your body. All the markings will be done on the mask, and the radiation goes right through it."

"How long will I have to undergo radiation?"

"I can't say for certain until I've done my calculations." He makes a face as if he's about to calculate the entire solar system, and frankly looks as though he'd be able to.

"Why is it so complicated?"

"We want to spare your lungs as much as possible, and that means we'll need to direct the rays at you from the sides. I don't know if we'll be able to reach all the spots we need to."

"I'm sure you'll manage."

A friendly smile plays on Dr. N's mouth. His voice is calm and friendly, his demeanor modest and approachable. *So they do exist, considerate doctors.*

"That's the attitude we want. We start in two weeks."

My right lung and liver are going to be severely damaged and my esophagus hit as well. Radiation is nothing more than burning off unwanted tissue along with any wanted tissue that happens to be in the way. At every radiation session my cells get a good beating, after which they try to restore themselves. The idea is that the cancer cells give up the fight, while the healthy cells survive. Apparently, my body will figure all this out on its own. My clean left lung will take over breathing for the time being, and my liver will produce new tissue to make up for the damaged parts.

I thank Dr. N for being so positive. In two weeks the party starts, with a host of nasty new side effects: fatigue, pneumonitis, dry skin, fever, coughing, inability to swallow.

An hour later, I'm lying flat on my back. Two men are busy constructing a mold of my chest with a bucket of plaster and some spatulas and brushes. It takes hours but I endure them peacefully. On Mom—who's sitting next to me—they drew directly on the skin.

"The plaster will feel cold to start with," they warn me. I have to stay very still because it dries quickly. My chest in a full plaster cast, a bald head sticking out of the top, and men in white suits moving around me: I feel like I'm starring in a sci-fi movie.

TUESDAY, JULY 26

I close my suitcase. Annabel is waiting outside for me in the car that will take us to the airport. I had not expected my doctors to take into consideration the agenda of my social life, but Dr. N didn't find it a problem to start radiation five days later so I can enjoy some France.

We're in the hills above Saint-Tropez, parading along the waterfront. I'm drinking a noisette and a Kir Royale at the same time and leafing through a tacky, touristy beverage list in search of other delicacies. Nothing is too much on the Côte d'Azur. Sea creatures grilled and steamed in all shapes and sizes, extravagant drinks and desserts—we order it all.

I open my bag, rummage around for my sunglasses, and lose myself in my surroundings. What a mess. Armed with a giant parasol and a lifetime supply of sunscreen, I make my way through the gorgeous, tanned bodies on Pampelonne beach.

Pam is enjoying the sea breeze. I didn't think I would be able to enjoy this summer, the liberating feeling of driving along a coastal road in the sunshine. I can't tell where the sea ends and the sky begins. The sun is shining like mad and I just want to soak it up, but I have to get back in the shade before Nurse Pauke finds me and scolds me. I wouldn't be surprised to find her here somewhere, keeping an eye on me. Hidden beneath a huge sun hat and a pair of Jackie O sunglasses, I smear on another layer of SPF 50 sunscreen. *So much for feeling the sun on my skin.* Lucky Annabel is lying beside me working on her tan. I have to get my tan from a bottle this summer. All around me I see magic lotions and creams promising me a beautiful, natural-looking tan. I've tried them all: foams to be applied with rubber gloves (ever since in surprisingly short supply in the oncology department), sprays, creams, gels, and lotions. None of them do for me what the sun does for Annabel.

I watch the boats dotting the blue ocean. Their sails an amazing white, the ocean an amazing blue. As I stare into the water, the world of the hospital seems a million miles away. I look farther, focus harder, and my nightmares disappear. I close my eyes—nothing there either. I'm floating away, all my fears forgotten. When I open my eyes again, all I see is blue.

"What's that?" Annabel points at something drifting on the waves. It's drifting farther and farther away.

I take a quick look but can't really be bothered to see what she's talking about. "I'm sure it's nothing," I murmur. I lay my head back down, listening to the sound of the waves breaking. A soft sea breeze caresses my head. It feels good, comforting. It must be this Mediterranean sun that makes it feel so soothing. Suddenly, Annabel sits up straight.

"Weren't you wearing a wig before?" She lets out a scream. "Sophie, it's Pam! In the water!" Annabel sprints into the sea to save Pam from drowning.

* * *

The blue sky slowly turns pink, the first boats start sailing back inland, and lights are flickering on. As evening falls, we swap our sandals for high heels.

We end up at a party in the garden of some ridiculously wealthy American movie producer, somewhere in the hills above Saint-Tropez. Annabel and I have always had good luck when it comes to these kinds of things. Tonight we happened to be in the right place at the right time to squeeze in with the rest. Just when we were driving down toward the coast, we saw everybody heading up. We looked around, recognized a face, used the person's name to get in, and here we are.

"Champagne?"

"Yes. Why not?"

Among the long-legged Russians and short-legged Arabs I let myself go. I love garden parties, even if I do feel a little out of place as the chemo sweat runs down my back and my wig dances along to its own rhythm. Luckily my fake tan is reasonably believable and there are no telltale smears ruining my cleavage.

The whole party is a parade of people flashing their money. We spot Paris Hilton, with the longest legs and the most complicated strappy sandals I have ever seen. Dresses straight from the pages of *Vogue*. Countless beautiful women and an impressive number of beautiful men. An old cowboy from Los Angeles. Ivana Trump, Catherine Deneuve, and Natalia Vodianova. Annabel and I look at each other and smile giddily.

At two A.M. we're exhausted. Me from my low blood count; Annabel from her precariously high heels. We sink down on the steps to the balcony and watch all that glitters pass by.

These are the little perks of having cancer: after your dreams have been swapped away all you need to be happy at two A.M. are some fresh cool steps with your best friend next to you.

* * *

The next day I wake up with a scalp covered with bites. I had thought to be liberated from the mosquitos this year with all the chemo in my blood, but they still prefer me over Annabel. Wearing a wig only makes it worse. I guess I'm doomed to a scarf. What a drag.

I take a cold shower to wash away the itchiness. I do have to admit: the feeling of fresh drops on my bald head is priceless.

WEDNESDAY, AUGUST 10

Back home, Rob stands behind me, giving me a big hug. We're in the health food store—unmistakable with its huge tubs of vitamins, boxes of herbal remedies, and loads of Asian shoppers. I'm reading a pamphlet about menopause. The symptoms are scarily similar to the nasty side effects of the chemo: hot flashes and missed periods. My periods stopped coming when the chemo started. Twenty-two and bled out already. My herb guide says aniseed has been known to revive menstruation. We order a shopping bag full.

FRIDAY, AUGUST 12

Rob sits next to me in the car as we pull into the hospital grounds in Rotterdam. He's a little sweaty as well, but for a different reason: last night's vodka.

Rita, who came for free with the radiation, is my favorite taxi driver. She opens the window a notch and carefully follows the signs to radiation. For the next seven weeks, I have to go down to Rotterdam for a daily session. On average, that means three hours on the road for ten minutes of radiation. Which means chatting with Rita and taking naps in the backseat. My parents often go with me. If it were up to them, they would come every day. Often one of my friends or Rob tags along. But sometimes I just like being alone with Rita.

In the radiation room, wearing a spotless white coat, is Kevin. He's always friendly and never too busy for a chat while setting up the machine. I must look as though I could use some distraction. He means well, but it's no use. I'm in my own sci-fi movie. Green laser beams and red dots shoot out of a mechanical trunk the size of a whale revolving around my bald head. I'm strapped to a narrow table, my upper body naked and wrapped in a plaster mask with an incomprehensible series of marks drawn on it.

Kevin presses the hooks of my thorax mask into the table and then turns to the machine moaning and groaning above me. A loud noise; the machine is ready to go and slowly starts to move. Electronic humming and invisible rays. The enemy within me is under attack, but all I feel is my arms, which are starting to hurt from being held outstretched above my head.

In the waiting room a dozen other heroes are waiting for their turn with the evil machine—all with their own scripts and fight scenes. One of them is a young boy, maybe eight or nine years old. He's tough and vulnerable at the same time. He has this alien look to him, bald and no eyebrows and all.

He doesn't want to come back. I heard him telling one of the white coats. "The big machine hurts," he said.

I look at him and feel my eyes welling with tears. I wish I could tell him that this is all a movie set. That the men in white coats are on his side, and that the good guys always win. I want to tell him that he'll win the battle, and then he can go back to playing with his friends. I feel an overwhelming desire to talk to him, but I don't know how. I open my mouth but nothing comes out. His name is called and we both disappear behind different doors.

MONDAY, AUGUST 29

I'm walking down the beach at Wijk aan Zee, a small village on the North Sea. The wet sand sticks to my toes. It's a game between sea and sand; the cool water rinses my feet clean, then the beach attaches itself to me all over again. I walk from left to right—east to west—but that can't be right, I realize, when I see the factory pipes of IJmuiden appear on my left-hand side. A few meters further up, Jan's dog, Ben, is happily running along to the rhythm of the tennis ball that Rob keeps throwing. I'm busy looking for shells. Every time the sea retreats, I enthusiastically sift through the surf and then empty my findings into Jan's oversize yellow tank top, which I've stolen and am using as a pouch. I even find a few shells with holes worn into them, one big enough to slip onto my necklace. Now I have two shells decorating my neck: one from the waves in the South of France and one from Wijk aan Zee.

I collect shells from every place I visit. I put them in my shower, next to the sink, or on my shelves filled with tea lights. I use them to store jewelry and other treasures. Sometimes, in the rare moments when I let myself dream, I fantasize about living in a beach house, with the beach as my back garden. My desk would be facing the sea: endless views to stretch my thoughts. I'm still writing every day; it has become as much a part of me as my illness. Jan is the only person who reads and comments on all my words, and there are some I handed out to Mom and Dad and Sis. Some things are easier written than said.

The wind blows furiously and Blondie's hair knots up like crazy. We leave the beach to eat somewhere overlooking the water. I have a goat cheese salad with multicolored tomatoes while I sift through the day's findings. Rob is calculating the angle at which he will get the most sun to tan his face. Jan is rummaging through his bag full of newspapers as his dog hassles the neighbors. I go off to the bathroom to sort out my hair with the antique silver brush that belonged to my late grandmother. It's the only brush that works with synthetic hair.

TUESDAY, SEPTEMBER 6

Rob and I sit at the kitchen table discussing "our future". The boyfriend conversation. Yagh. We're happy together, but more as friends than as lovers. We're living in this strange situation in which there's only today. And today Rob is what I want. Or well, Jurriaan is who I really want but I can't have him. In the moments I allow myself to look further, I know that Rob and I aren't going to make it. He fits my life like a glove though. He's best friends with Jochem and Jan, and so am I. But we've never completely gone for it, and I don't think I would in different circumstances (read If I had been healthy or if Jurriaan had wanted me). Being together is a choice, according to Rob, and one we both prefer to postpone until a time when we can actually talk about a future.

I wished so often for two strong arms to hold me at night when the lights are out, when I'm all alone with my fear. But now they're here, I don't know how to let them hold me. I still feel like an island in his arms, no matter how close I cuddle up to him.

WEDNESDAY, SEPTEMBER 14

It's the longest traffic jam in the Netherlands and we're right at the end of it, en route from my chemo in Amsterdam to my radiation in Rotterdam. Sis is with me today. The longer the drive, the longer I sleep—that's one advantage to this mess. After half an hour of chatting, I fall asleep on her lap, exhausted and fed up. I don't want to be a sci-fi heroine anymore, I'm done playing tough. I'm frail and flimsy. My stomach and cheeks are hollowed out. The look in my eyes is unfocused and the pink skin around them is now puffy and dark. The scale has never been this low: there's only fifty-one kilos left of me. Sis gently strokes my soft head with her fingertips; Pam is lying next to me on the seat. For the rest of the drive Sis strokes my arms and back with her soft fingers. She knows how much I love that.

Suddenly I feel something running between my legs. I quickly press my hand against my crotch to stop the stream.

"Sis?"

"Yes?"

"I'm peeing."

"Oh shit."

"It's okay, it's already stopped. I think only my pants are wet."

Sis breaks the silence. "Granny." We both burst out laughing, which makes me pee again.

What a mess.

THURSDAY, SEPTEMBER 15

"Miss van der Stap."

I look up, straight into the eyes of my own Dr. McDreamy. Leaning toward me, his hands folded, he looks at me intently with those blue eyes. I blush and feel a new hot flash coming on fast, along my back, leaving behind a trail of sweat. This menopause business is starting to get ridiculous.

"What can I do for you?" he asks.

If he only knew.

"Time for a lung test?"

I'm spending the afternoon visiting Dr. K, blowing and sighing into his tubes. I wonder what his life outside of the hospital looks like. Just like everyone else probably. But he must take his fair share of baggage home with him. Maybe he whiles away most of his worries on the way home, but no doubt he takes a few to bed with him. I wonder if I'm one of the things he takes to bed. The thought excites me. But what does he think about? Is it just sympathy? Does he secretly long for me the way I long for him?

Too bad Rob has followed my example and found another object to look at as well. Although I'm the one who encouraged him to see other women, I hate hearing about the one he chose to see and would prefer not to know of her existence. She does come up every now and then, of course. Sometimes because I can't contain my curiosity, other times because Rob has this idea that as friends we should be able to share this kind of thing. *Yeah, right.*

MONDAY, OCTOBER 10

This morning I finished the book *Oscar and the Lady in Pink* by Éric-Emmanuel Schmitt. Oscar is ten years old and has leukemia. He lives his entire life within the walls of the hospital, where he and the other children fall asleep each night and wake up each morning. Just like me, Oscar has a favorite nurse: Mamie-Rose. She's the one who advises Oscar to direct his questions to God. So Oscar begins writing letters to God and finds a new friend, without realizing that, as the days go by, he's really answering his own questions.

Oscar has various friends in the hospital. His best friends are Einstein and Popcorn. He explains that Einstein isn't called that because he's so smart but because his head is two times the size of the other kids. That's my kind of humor. Popcorn owes his nickname to his obesity. Oscar says the only piece of clothing that fits him—barely—is an American baseball shirt with stripes. The shirt is so tight that the stripes are not going down straight anymore and it makes Oscar feel seasick. Oscar prefers to spend time with the two girls on his ward: Chinese Girl and Peggy Blue. The first wears a wig in the style of a Chinese girl, and the second always looks blue because of her medicine. Oscar has a nickname too: "Bald Egg."

Mamie-Rose spends a lot of time at Oscar's bedside. She amuses him with exciting stories of her former boxing career and talks about Oscar's illness and death as easily as she talks about life and growing old. She teaches Oscar to see his inevitable death as part of his life and reminds him that one day she, too, will die, just as he will, very soon. The doctors have given him less than two weeks. It's Mamie-Rose who teaches Oscar how to grow up from a young boy of ten to an old man of a hundred in his last days on Earth, a man who makes peace with the idea of never waking up.

Maybe Oscar died so young so that his story would live on. For his loved ones, for his friends in the ward, for people like me, for all those other Oscars—little people but big heroes. I'm positive Oscar is not invented. That he really lived, really felt seasick and that he really passed away.

THURSDAY, OCTOBER 20

I blink and feel my eyelashes brush against the pillowcase. Ever since I switched to maintenance chemo rather than full weeks in the hospital, my hair has slowly begun growing back. My lashes. My eyebrows. And, unfortunately, all the rest too. Back to shaving and plucking and waxing. I get up and go in search of mascara, hidden somewhere in the bottom of my makeup case. I'm also sporting a light fuzz on my head now, which brings some character back to my face.

I have no appetite for breakfast, lunch, or dinner, but that seems to be normal for radiation patients. My body responds directly to every treatment and sometimes in such extremes: I've gone from emaciated to blowfish, then back to a normal weight, and now I look anorexic again. It's exhausting. I'm as energetic as a squeezed-out lemon.

Despite all our reservations—and admittedly due to some jealousy on my side—Rob and I have gone away for a few days. To Luxembourg: lakes, mountains, fresh air. I take hundreds of photos of autumn leaves, Rob, archways, Rob, panoramas, more Rob.

In the morning I wander out of the hotel as Pam; at night I crawl into bed as Uma. The receptionist is confused and looks at Rob with a questioning gaze.

"Got tired of the blonde, left her in town," Rob says. That playful threat makes me enjoy each look, each joke, and each touch even more.

We eat cheese, drink red wine, and pet friendly dogs in the street. We go out dancing. Well, Rob dances; I sit and look. We admire the mountains and eat chocolate. It's romantic and beautiful, but still I wonder if we're not better as friends than as lovers. I don't know if it's the cancer or if it's us, but Luxembourg seems to be telling us that it's not meant to be. I wish I knew more about love. I wish I knew why my love stories never seem to last.

"Look at these great pictures!" I exclaim in the car on the way back to Amsterdam. Rob and Sue at breakfast, Rob and Pam in the car, Rob and Uma wandering around town, Rob and Blondie at dinner. *Fuck. Letting go is hard.*

WEDNESDAY, OCTOBER 26

"Does that mean you might move to Hong Kong *permanently*?"

"I have no idea, anything could happen. But yes, it is a possibility."

"Do you know how far away that is?"

"We'll get used to it."

"I'm sorry, but I can't let you go there. I just can't."

Sis holds back her tears. She is curled up close beside me; I'm in my standard position, tired and sick, tucked up in bed.

"I'm sorry, Sis, I know it's not a choice. You found your man. You have to go."

"I just can't bear the thought of leaving you. Especially not now."

"Can't Kieran find something to do here?"

"Sophie, I won't go if … you know." I know what she means, but neither of us can say it out loud.

I hug her tightly. "That means you're going. 'If' doesn't exist. I will get better."

Sis quickly wipes away a tear.

* * *

I sit in front of my screen waiting for the words to fill up the white space. It's been days since I've written a word. And just when I was starting to get the hang of it. Can't say I like my life today. Frankly, it sucks. Fucking cancer. Fucking Hong Kong.

SUNDAY, NOVEMBER 6

Dad came up with the idea to get some fresh air, and a thirty-minute drive to the beach wasn't far enough. So here we are, driving along the mountain roads of the Sierra Nevada.

"You'll see. You'll love it. Otto immediately offered his help when he heard the news. He's a renowned doctor, you see. And Bebé is a sweetheart. They now live in a very quiet mountain village."

Otto has convinced my father that the fresh air will do wonders. I remember Otto. As a child I was always a bit scared of him. No, that sounds too nice. Actually I was scared shitless of him. There was something in the way he looked at us. I haven't seen him since. It's the first time I will meet Bebé. When Dad suggested we go and see them together, I didn't know what to think of it. But then, I'm not a child anymore and I'd love to see some mountains and stars.

Otto and Bebé have both been married three times. Third time's the charm, they say. Together they must be doubly charmed. He and Bebé emigrated to Spain five years ago, to the region of Andalusia. After years of hard work as a general surgeon, then plastic surgeon, and then electrical engineer, he was fed up with life in the city.

Born in Zimbabwe into an English family, Bebé started modeling quite young and has lived through the infamous London of the sixties, quite an exciting life, sharing rooms with Twiggy, cooking dinners for the Rolling Stones, dancing with the Beatles. So exciting, in fact, that each and every day here she enjoys the peace and quiet she and Otto have found in Spain. They live their lives isolated from the rest of the world. The nearest village is several kilometers away, and it doesn't amount to much. But that remoteness is why they love living here, and why I enjoy it so much. The simplicity of one market, one village café, and one church. The surroundings are spectacular: a deep valley below, mountains above, and a sliver of ocean in the distance. Best part: can't find any trace of my childhood fear for Otto. And Bebé really is a sweetheart. Dad hadn't exaggerated this time.

Time does not exist here. We get up when we want to get up, we eat when we want to eat, and we plan what we want to plan. Which isn't much more than a visit to the local market or a day out in nearby Granada. I forget what it is like to feel time slipping away. Usually, even if I lose track of the days, I'm aware of the year passing by as I count down my fifty-four weeks of chemo. As I cross off each week, I understand more and more what the concept of today means.

The end of my chemotherapy is slowly approaching, and I know I should be happy, but what will I do without chemo? What if my tumors always stay a part of me?

At least Otto's medical background makes me feel safe while I'm here. We discuss my file (which I still drag along to every doctor I meet), my experience with doctors, which medicines I'm on, and the horrible statistics. They show me how to test my urine for my frequent bladder infections (another unexpected side effect of the treatment) by peeing in a pot, and they tell me which vitamins and supplements to take to tackle them.

Before bed, I take my medicine and swallow extra vitamin C to combat the bladder infection I can feel coming on. Then I snuggle deep under the blankets.

Rest, rest, rest.

TUESDAY, NOVEMBER 8

I push Lydia's hair aside so that it doesn't hang down in my plate of fish and vegetables. Lydia is my latest addition. She was given to me today by Bebé, a souvenir from when she used to wear wigs back in the sixties. Lydia's warm auburn hair fits me perfectly here in the Andalusian landscape.

We are having dinner in the local village and talking about doctors, medicine, and my cancer, which has been given many diagnoses by many different pathologists. Otto—who treats me like a daughter since the day I stepped into his house—thinks there's a chance I was misdiagnosed, and that the faulty diagnosis might well have saved my life. That I may be "overtreated," but that I could otherwise have been "undertreated," in which case I would be dead as a doorknob. He explains that there are so many unknown elements swimming around in my body that the area between sickness and health is rather gray. What an enlightening conversation. *Such fun, talking to doctors.*

I fall asleep under a blanket of stars.

WEDNESDAY, NOVEMBER 9

The next morning I wake up early and decide to go for a walk. The stars are all gone, now it's Mount Lugar to surprise me with nature's beauty. The dogs start barking when I open the door and follow me over the path along the river. I take a left turn at a beautiful fig tree, just like Bebé told me to do yesterday over dinner. Here the path becomes steeper, taking me through an empty ruin accompanied by an enormous palm tree and then bringing me to the acacia. The air is so fresh here. And although it's November, the sun warms my face, heating up my muscles. I walk up the ridge of Mount Lugar, overlooking another valley. I try to have happy thoughts or no thoughts at all, but I can't forget about Oscar and Marco. Marco died exactly a year ago. Although I never knew him, I think of him as I go to bed. It fits in with my own funereal thoughts. It almost feels rude to write about Marco without ever having met him. But it feels even ruder not to write about him, to forget him. To me he is not forgotten. I carry his picture with me in my wallet; I wear the yellow bracelet his father gave me. He is a part of my thoughts. Tomorrow in the village church I'll light a candle for Marco and Oscar. And for my own mom, dad, and sister, who have had to deal with so much these past months.

Surely I won't be one of the ones who doesn't make it?

I hear footsteps approaching. "So this is where you are!"

"Morning, Dad."

"How did you sleep?"

"Like a rock. You were right. It was a great idea to come here. Breathing even comes easier to me here."

"Then Otto was right. Good, that's good. Would you care for some breakfast?"

"Well, actually, yes." My stomach makes a rumbling sound. I haven't been hungry for breakfast in months.

"Great. But first let this old man get back on his feet. It's quite a walk to get here."

FRIDAY, NOVEMBER 18

Today is the fourth day I haven't seen or spoken to Rob. He's off with his new love interest, with whom he might be super happy and in love. Today sucks.

On my agenda? I'm back at the hospital for my chemo. Toeing the line between life and death. That does put Rob in second place in my thoughts. For now. I guess that's something to be cheerful about.

There are six green recliners next to me; I'm in the seventh. When I came in they were all occupied, now there are three that are empty. Pauke is always here, which automatically gives her authority over the other nurses, who are part-time nurses. And she has a glass jar filled with ladyfingers on her desk. That helps too. I don't understand why they keep on trying to feed us sugar as every but seriously every diet book about cancer tells you that it feeds on sugar. In some ways this place where miracles happen is incredibly backwards.

Dr. L usually stops by when I'm here. He comes to see the day patients only when they have complaints or questions, both are almost always the case with me.

WEDNESDAY, NOVEMBER 23

"Are you in love?" I look at Rob fearfully, preparing myself for the blow that will undoubtedly come.

"Sophie ..."

It hurts. I want it to hurt less than when I heard my diagnosis, because love is supposed to be less hard to deal with than death, and maybe it is, but I don't know as I already seem to have forgotten the pain of that day. Selective memory.

Rob looks straight ahead. He tries to touch me, hold my hand, stroke my cheek. I push him away. *Goddamn it, this hurts!* I want to touch him, to feel his arms and his body around me, but I can't. I scream that he has to leave, to get out of my life, and to take the pain he's caused with him. I say that I never want to see him again, and right now I really believe it. I forget that it was me who pushed him away.

THURSDAY, NOVEMBER 24

I sit on Annabel's windowsill, wrapped in a dressing gown, after waking up next to her early this morning. I look outside and feel totally shitty. Shitty because I slept curled up against Annabel and not Rob, who instead probably spent the night snuggling with someone else. And shitty because my next scan is approaching fast and I'm scared.

I hate everything. The whole month of December with all its traditions: Sinterklaas, Christmas, New Year's—I'm dreading it all. The family dinners, the endless appetizers, the oysters and champagne. I hate myself for having pushed Rob away and now being heartbroken. I hate how I long for his arms more than Annabel's, because hers are always there for me. I hate the stabbing pains in my body that make me think I'm dying. I hate my stupid tumor and his whole stupid family. I hate my body. I hate my life.

I look at the clock impatiently. I make myself another cup of tea and sit watching the second hand ticking off the next eight minutes. I have a plan. I reach for the phone and ring my doctors' offices in Amsterdam and Rotterdam. I convince both my doctors to move up the date of the scan. I exaggerate the stabbing pains just a little bit. I tell them I'm feeling worse than usual. How can I explain to them that the pain and the uncertainty are so much worse without Rob? And how do I explain that to my parents, my sister, and the rest of my terrified family? Sis will understand. I call her, and after half an hour on the phone with her I'm still sobbing. She's crying too.

"Why don't you come and stay with us tonight? Kieran will be home late. We can watch movies together. Maybe Mom wants to join in too."

After hanging up I call Mom, who was just called by the hospital because my phone line was busy. I have some explaining to do.

"Mom?"

"Hi, honey, how are you feeling?" She sounds caring and worried.

"Not so good. I've moved up my scan. I can't take the uncertainty. Not without Rob."

"I understand, sweetheart. The hospital just called to say the scan is now on Wednesday the 30th. Can I come?"

"I don't know. I want Jur to come. I'll have to see if he can make it."

"Okay. Are you coming home soon? I'll make a pot of tea."

"I'll be there soon. Thanks, Mom."

* * *

When I arrive home, Mom is reading the newspaper at the kitchen table. She's waiting for me with a big pot of tea.

"Hi, dear," she says while filling my cup.

"Hi, Mom."

"Did you speak to Jur?"

"Left him a message."

She looks at me tenderly.

"You don't disapprove of me moving up the scan?" It's the last scan and the most important one: everything needs to be gone now.

"Darling, of course not. The uncertainty can be worse than the cancer. I know breaking up with Rob has been tough on you. A few days more or less won't change the diagnosis. Otherwise your doctors wouldn't have agreed to reschedule it. If it gives you peace of mind, it's worth it."

"Thanks for understanding." I look at her, trying to suss out what she's thinking. "Are you scared that the cancer will come back?"

"My cancer?"

"Yes."

"Yes, I'm still scared sometimes. You've done a good job of helping me forget about my own worries this past year, but so many women don't make it. I try to stay positive."

"That's not always easy," I say. I look up at her, suddenly realizing that she has been here for me all that time without asking for anything in return. I completely forgot about her cancer.

"It's bloody difficult." Mom looks at me warmly. Her eyes are moist. She's doing her best to keep her tears from me. Now that I look at her, I realize she's been keeping her tears from all of us since the beginning. Just as I did so many times last year when our roles were reversed. I couldn't imagine being any closer to her than I am, but we still hide our tears. We act stronger than we are. Maybe by fooling the outside world, we fool ourselves.

"Mom, when this is all over, let's promise to go to all our future checkups together."

"I'd love that, Sophie."

"Me too."

Finally we both cry. Our hands reaching for one another across the kitchen table.

That evening Mom, Sis, and I curl up on the sofa watching *Pride and Prejudice*. Three different women who, when watching Jane Austen, are one and the same. They all want Mister Darcy.

FRIDAY, NOVEMBER 25

Thanks to Jan, I've been invited to the offices of the Amsterdam-based urban magazine *NL20*, a hip cultural publication that knows everything worth doing in the city. Jan sent them some of my writing, and the editors at *NL20* invited me for an interview. The young man sitting opposite me nods his head, making his dreadlocks swing in front of his face.

"I like your writing samples. The wigs give you a unique approach. If you can turn your wig-wearing adventures into journalism, I think it could really be something. We'll try it out for the next two months, and if it goes well, we can talk about something more permanent."

On the outside Uma plays it cool, but inside I'm jumping up and down. I never imagined cancer as an asset.

A gay guy in a multicolored Adidas tracksuit walks by.

"Oh my God, I loooove your hair!" he exclaims, accompanied by theatrical hand gestures. After a few months and several nights out Uma is starting to get frizzy and looks more and more hippie. I kind of like it.

I smile in response, without really knowing what to say. I'm still a bit dumbstruck.

"This is Louis. He does the agenda and a few other bits and pieces, such as The Fitting Room."

"The Fitting Room?"

"He picks people from the street and asks them about their personal style."

"Not just anyone," Louis clarifies, "only the stylish. Last week it was an Afghani girl in a flower-print burka."

"Ah. Burka fashion. Very stylish."

"As you can probably tell, the atmosphere here is pretty relaxed," Dreadlocks continues. I look around. He's not exaggerating. Dreadlocks is barefoot and wearing a Hawaiian floral-print shirt. Louis is holding a Ping-Pong paddle in his hand. It's silly. I love silly.

"You'll have my first column next week." I'm so excited; I start writing as soon as I get home.

MONDAY, NOVEMBER 28

The woman sitting opposite me keeps silent. She listens, takes notes, sighs. Occasionally she interrupts me, but only when I get lost in my own words. On her advice I bought two books: *The Healing Journey* and *Getting Well Again*, both written by Dr. O. Carl Simonton. The idea is to visualize your cancer cells and then visualize a shark or whatever you like swimming around and have him eat them.

I guess cancer can make you kind of desperate.

So I opened up Google and went looking for a therapist specializing in Simonton methodology. I've never seen one before.

It was Mom who advised me to see someone. Even though she sent away the hospital psychologist after one session when she was ill—my mom is kind of picky—the experience did encourage her to talk to a friend who has her own practice. Since we cried together that day at the kitchen table, I feel closer to her than ever.

The woman asks me to visualize my fear with my eyes closed and then draw it on a sheet of paper. I draw a cloud using blue and green, with another cloud above it that I try with all my might to push away, but it beats me and merges into my first cloud.

She asks me to close my eyes again and to describe my drawing. "What happens next?"

"I'm hanging it, in a frame above my bed."

"And?"

"I walk over, lift it off the nail, and go back to bed, holding the frame close to me like a stuffed animal."

"What do you think that means?"

"That I'm a sadomasochist cuddling my fear?"

"Sophie, there is more than one Sophie in you: a happy Sophie, a strong Sophie, but also a frightened and insecure Sophie. You need to accept that before you can move on."

"So maybe it's trying to say I don't need to push away my fear?"

"Maybe."

The key concepts I take away from our sessions are "cleaning up" and "clearing out."

"Can I come back tomorrow?"

"Yes, Sophie, you can."

I feel like hugging her on my way out. After all, we shared so much. But that's not what therapists do. Instead, I give her a formal hand shake.

TUESDAY, NOVEMBER 29

I want to rip Rob to shreds. I sift through my phone contacts looking for old flings, potential crushes. Anything to avoid sitting alone on my couch.

Maybe a new hairstyle will help. A new identity that doesn't belong to him in any way. Maybe being a new me will help me forget the old me who's in love with Rob. Or maybe he'll fall madly in love with me again when he sees me looking newly beautiful and intriguing. At the theater shop I go for daring, platinum-blonde locks that go down to my waist. A little bit exotic, a lot sexy: perfect for my new single status. I call her Bebé as a tribute to Bebé in Andalusia. Then I buy some new makeup to match my new hair: black eyeliner and purple eye shadow. *Let the feast begin.*

Is he having sex with her right now? *Asshole. I hope he falls out of bed and hurts himself.*

On my way to the grocery store I pass Café Finch, where we both like to go. And there behind the window I see him sitting with a girl with very long legs. They're laughing. I watch them for a long second, take a deep breath, then hide behind Bebé and walk on.

One more day until the final scan.

WEDNESDAY, NOVEMBER 30

I'm sitting in the same chair I was the day I got my bad news. Beside me is Jur. I asked him to come today because he's the only one who can look me in the eye and convince me that anything is possible. Even when the doctors say it isn't.

Across the desk is Dr. L. He smiles. "What have you got on your head this time? Pretty, that long hair."

It's the first time that I have done the scan and get results the same day. My heart lifts as the fear in the pit of my stomach slowly lessens. His friendliness is a good sign. I nod and tug at Bebé's hair nervously. I've done my makeup and am wearing my prettiest blouse, which Otto and Bebé gave me, all aimed at turning my hope into conviction.

"Well, Sophie, I have good news for you."

I see pride and happiness in my doctor's eyes. My hand jerks up in an automatic spasm of joy, looking for Jur's hand. His hand does the same. I thought I would jump up and hug Dr. L—that's what happens in the scene I've played out a hundred times in my mind. But I just bend over his desk and kiss him on the cheek as a tear rolls down my own.

"The scans look good. Great, actually. Nothing left to see. You are what we call 'X-ray clean.'"

"How clean is that?"

"Well, we can't be completely sure. Although there are no visible abnormalities, we can never guarantee that you are one hundred percent clean. Time will tell."

Outside of the office, Jur interrupts my questions with a big kiss and a long, comforting embrace. "What a load of rubbish," he says as we leave the hospital. "You're clean! Forget all that crap about 'time will tell.'"

I'm so glad Jur is here. He would know.

I feel a rush of love not only for this amazing boy in front of me, but also for Annabel and Jan and even Rob. For my neighbors. For my family. *Clean, clean, clean.* This is better than a triple orgasm! My God, what a joy it is to be cured. I just can't believe it; I'm scared that the joy is too good to be true. When it comes to life, I've become a bit mistrusting. But that doesn't take the feeling away. I immediately call home, hear Mom sob for the very last time, and walk with Jur into a café to celebrate.

Three glasses of wine and a few tapas later, I walk down the street to a restaurant on the Prinsengracht to meet up with Annabel and continue the celebration. The wine and the good news have gone straight to my head. Annabel is outside waiting for me and I fall into her arms. I can't believe it. *Am I really clean? Cured? Is this it?* I look at the people around me with jobs and schedules and plans. *Am I one of them again?*

THURSDAY, DECEMBER 1

At midnight I walk into Sugar Factory, a new club. I'm going out dancing, this time to remember and not to forget. Although my heart is still beating as fast as it was in Dr. L's office, I've managed to stick on my enormous fake eyelashes and to draw a smooth line around my eyelids. I'm wearing super-high-heeled boots, Bebé's long blonde hair, and a sexy caftan that barely covers my butt. Annabel is wearing jeans and a tight jacket, and her dark hair is in a long ponytail. Jur is dressed in a green T-shirt, chunky black Nikes, and baggy jeans. He looks even cuter than he did yesterday. We drink red wine, just like yesterday. And like tomorrow and the day after tomorrow.

But he doesn't look. Not in the direction of my lips, at least. He talks, listens, answers, makes jokes, and speaks of his ex-girlfriend, his lovers. All while being terribly attractive.

What about me? As I look at him, I think about my lips and his lips. My hips and his hips. My legs wrapped around his legs, and my eggs on toast next to his eggs on toast on Sunday morning. I fantasize that we'll spend my post-chemo year on white beaches and in unknown cities, but mostly under my sheets and his.

In the ladies' room I apply some extra gloss to my lips. I pull my blonde hair into place and undo an extra button.

But he doesn't look. He's caught up in his own busy love life and doesn't seem to notice that I'm waiting in line as well.

"Jur?"

"Yes?"

"I've told you how much I like you, right?" He's walked me home and now we're standing outside of my house. The perfect setting for a Hollywood kiss.

Jur looks a little confused. "Yes?"

"Well, I've been a little in love with you from the first day we met. I mean, not all day every day because I don't see you as much as I would like, but I can't help it, I really like you."

"Oh, uh, wow. That's really honest of you." Not the response I was looking for.

"And?" I bat my XXL lashes for added effect.

"Sophie, you know I have a girlfriend."

"Yes I do. But I had to tell you anyway."

"Sophie, I think you're amazing, and we do have something special, but I think we're better as friends."

"Oh."

"Come here, you." Jur grabs ahold of me and gives me a big hug.

Great, just what I wanted. Another friend.

FRIDAY, DECEMBER 2

It's party time. The ecstatic feeling from the good news is still raging through my body. I can't sleep. I'm lying in bed with my eyes wide-open. It's time to start getting ready anyway. Off to Club NL to celebrate.

Sis is joining the party too. Even Rob is here, and he greets me with a long kiss. Seeing him again, I instantly realize I want to stay friends with him no matter what, so I do my best not to think about Lady Long Legs. Much easier with her away on vacation.

Rob and I are together all night. We talk and talk. How much we care about each other. How sorry he is. How we'll be friends forever. Etc.

So now we're friends. Lucky me with all these great friends.

SATURDAY, DECEMBER 3

Now that I have a future again, things are looking up. Although the relief is immense, I'm still adjusting to the "ex" part of "ex-cancer patient." I open *NL20* and go in search of my column. It's my first piece, and therefore longer than usual: just introducing me needs nine pictures alone. The boys are by my side and they are as excited as I am. It's the first time that Rob and I are sharing the same terrace again. After two weeks without each other's company, it feels more than good to have him next to me, holding my hand. All we need to do is forget the existence of Lady Long Legs.

SOPHIE'S WIGS, it says at the top of the page. Below the headline they selected four out of the nine photos of me: the one with my middle fingers raised, which Jan took in the very beginning, and one each with Platina, Uma, and Sue. Random pictures that friends made.

The column I wrote is about my night with Tie Boy, which I always thought would remain completely anonymous. I wonder if he'll read it.

"Hey, look, I'm making my photography debut as well!" Rob points to the picture of Uma, which he took three months ago. I read the article out loud, and with every word, Rob's smile grows. Our hands make a ball that we don't let go.

"Rob, when are you going to get over this nonsense with Lady Long Legs? I can have her kidnapped, you know. Or, even better, attacked by a wild baboon. I have connections, you know."

"You take her feet, I'll take her by her head," Jan says, joining in the conversation. Rob laughs. The electric tension doesn't go away. We might have left each other, but it feels like our chemistry hasn't left us. For whatever reason, tonight it isn't hurting me as much as it has been. I feel great as I look at my journalistic debut on the coffee table. What a week: from cancer patient to feature article in a magazine.

MONDAY, DECEMBER 5

Today is a nostalgic day: Sinterklaas. Sinterklaas is a Dutch tradition that makes small kids very happy and their parents somewhat less so. It basically means that we get Christmas twice. Sinterklaas comes on the fifth of December. Just like Santa Claus, he's an old man handing out toys, only he rides his boat through Amsterdam rather than a flying sleigh. It requires a lot of holiday spirit to celebrate both Sinterklaas and Santa, so most parents make sure only one of them comes down the chimney.

Since we live on the canal, there are always boats passing by. Small private boats, rental boats, big tourist canal boats, and paddleboats. There's a number of houseboats tethered as well, most of them never moving. Fortunately, Sinterklaas's boat arrives at the very start of wintertime, when the canals aren't frozen yet. If we're lucky, the temperature will drop enough to make the canals freeze. Only one of the canals, the Keizersgracht, can be used for ice skating. The others stay open for boats. But it's magical when it happens. When we were kids, our winters were colder, and even our canal, the Herengracht, froze enough that boats couldn't get through.

This morning all the schoolkids from the other side of the canal have gathered to welcome their favorite holiday visitor. It's such a sweet sight, with the music playing traditional Sinterklaas carols. Sis and I stand in front of the window, overlooking the canal and watching a part of our childhood passing by. It's one of those moments that could be tearful, but we keep our eyes dry. It's surprising considering in a few hours my sister will be on a plane to the other side of the world. It's the downside to the tumors being gone.

She's leaving me.

I'm sad, but there's nothing we can do. She promised she's going to come back and visit often. Luckily her boyfriend works for an airline, which should ease the pain of flying back and forth. I'd much rather her come see me here in Amsterdam than me go visit her in Hong Kong. After everything I've been through this year, my travel bug has left me. I just want to be at home.

TUESDAY, DECEMBER 6

I'm not the only one who read last Saturday's edition of *NL20*. The daily talk show *De Wereld Draait Door* did too. Now they've invited me to come on the show and talk about it. Fortunately, Lady Long Legs is still somewhere far away and I have Rob all to myself. I'm glad he's with me; going on TV for the first time is scary, especially when wearing a wig.

In the makeup studio, all my various wigs are being passed around the room. I have brought matching outfits for all of them. Scarlet, followed by blonde, followed by brunette; short, long, straight, and platinum. Who shall it be? The makeup lady asks me which one is the most "me." *The most me? Good question. They're all me.*

Uma, Daisy, Blondie, Sue, or Platina? Bebé or Pam? Lydia? Stella, even? Who will come with me to sit between the hosts, the ironed shirts and clean-shaven faces, in front of the cameras, the media, and all those smiles? It sure is glam to be me. Glam to be a cancer patient.

The twenty minutes I was on live television are a complete blank to me. I don't remember how I walked up there. I don't even remember the questions they asked me. Or what I said. I do remember someone coming up to me just before I had to climb on stage saying another guest had bailed and I had to sit out the show—until the end. All of a sudden there were bright lights and the handsome host whose face I knew all too well sitting next to me. Then I started talking nonstop. And then, just as suddenly, it was over. When I turned around, Rob was all smiles and everyone else was congratulating me. An editor even handed me his card and told me he wants to turn my story into a book.

It's unreal. My wigs have become a media sensation. All I have to do is show people that you can live with cancer, that you can still laugh and enjoy yourself. That I still shop, dress up and go on dates. That those things are still just as much fun as they were before I got cancer, maybe even more so. That life with cancer doesn't have to be just an emaciated body, pain, and endless vomiting. And that wigs can be fun, and not just for me, but for anyone with cancer.

How's that for a business card? SOPHIE VAN DER STAP, THE GIRL WITH NINE WIGS.

When I get home from the studio, my inbox is full of e-mails. Ninety percent of the names are unknown to me, but from the subject lines I can see they are responses to the show. It makes me feel warm inside. My head doesn't hit the pillow until three thirty A.M.

One e-mail stands out:

Date: Tue, 6 Dec 20:39
From: Chantal
To: Sophie
Subject: hi Sophie

Just saw you on De Wereld Draait Door, a friend of mine called me to tell me to turn on the television. I'm a cancer patient like you, only a little older. Spread breast cancer. Not the best one to have either. It made me laugh to see the similarities between your attitude and mine. Especially when you talked about that guy in the club. I had a similar experience. You used your wig to hide the effects of chemo, and I always wear scarves to cover up the radiation marks on my chest. I told one guy they were road maps to find my G-spot ... A true desperate single, ha ha.

I never wore wigs. I only ever found one that I liked but it was too uncomfortable. I go through life with a baseball cap. People stare and whisper, and usually I just say, "This is what someone with cancer looks like." Not everyone appreciates my cynical humor, but I think you might.

Maybe you're thinking, hey, I want to get to know this girl or maybe the exact opposite, but I wanted to e-mail you because I think we have a lot in common. I bet you've received a thousand e-mails so I'll forgive you if you don't write back.

Love,

Chantal

WEDNESDAY, DECEMBER 7

"Are you there? Can you see me?" I ask.

"I can see you! Ready for the grand tour?"

"Hell yeah!"

I'm Skyping with Sis and she's about to show me her apartment in Hong Kong. The view is unbelievable. Absolutely everything looks high tech. And here I thought that Europe was the center of the universe. Not anymore, it seems.

"What do you think, will you be strong enough to come visit us soon?"

"Well, I still have two months of maintenance chemo. Maybe after, but I find it a bit scary to travel so far from Dr. L. I'd rather have him in arm's reach, you know?"

"I understand. Hong Kong isn't for the faint of heart—it's like a million people in one square meter and nobody looks where they're going. It makes me miss you even more."

"That's your fault for moving!" I reply. "I'm sorry. I can't help it. Didn't mean to say that."

"Yes you did."

"True." We both start laughing uncomfortably. "Well, the good thing is that I don't miss you yet, but it's only been two days."

Traveling has always been number one on my agenda, but now all I want to do is sit in the kitchen with the scent of soup simmering through the house. With Sis sitting next to me, Mom at the stove, and Dad reading his newspaper.

Hong Kong, Schmong Kong.

FRIDAY, DECEMBER 9

I lean back into one of the insanely uncomfortable seats for my day treatment at the hospital. A few hours ago the nurses welcomed me with cries of "Celebrity!" Sitting in the television studio, I'd forgotten about the IV drips and doctors. I'd forgotten my fears of the cancer coming back. I guess telly had its effect on me too. But now I have the headache from hell; it's as if a helicopter is zooming around in my head. Whenever my body suffers, fear lurks just around the corner. Oma, who's sitting next to me, doesn't seem to hear anything. I can tell by her eyes. She is smart, though, and sneaky so she confirms my remark about the noise of the propeller anyway, to make me feel better. The nurses look at me quizzically when I ask if they hear it. Some hospitals have helipads to receive medevac patients, but not this one.

"A helicopter?" the nurse asks again. "No, not in this hospital."

The yellow gunk has worked its way into my body; the empty bag is swinging back and forth uselessly from my IV pole.

"Yes, it sounds like a helicopter," I answer. I close my eyes and lean back. The IV needle is sticking out of my fake boob. Suddenly, everything goes dark and I'm close to passing out. Last Tuesday seems like a faraway dream, an outtake from the life of someone else. Now it's as if my body has remembered what's going on. The helicopter in my head is getting ready for takeoff, and I'm back to thinking about those who didn't make it.

SATURDAY, DECEMBER 10

Date: Sat, 10 Dec 12:32
From: Sophie
To: Chantal
Subject: Re: hi Sophie

Dear Chantal,

Thank you for your letter. I really enjoyed reading it.

Let's meet!

When is your next chemo? Shall we set up a date just in between our sessions if our chemo's match? (How nice to speak to a fellow cancer patient and not to have to explain why.)

In which neighborhood do you live?

Love,
Sophie

P.S. I very much appreciate your humor.

TUESDAY, DECEMBER 13

Jan convinced me that his chaotic schedule and my hospital appointments are a great excuse to flee the Amsterdam winter. He hates December with all the family holidays, so he keeps coming up with reasons we should take a trip this month. I think a lot of bad things happened to him during this month in the past, so he always flees. But I don't know the details. First, he was born in December, an event he's always been ambivalent about. Then his mother died in December when he still was a little boy. His father died too, but I don't know when. I do know he hates Christmas.

Because we usually think alike, we're off to Barcelona for a few days. At first I was hesitant and didn't feel like the journey at all. I'm still mostly homebound. But then I looked at Jan and saw us strolling on a sunny beach, getting lost in the small city lanes, and agreed. Although he's sixty and I'm twenty, we're pretty much on the same level, and even when we're not, it doesn't matter. We can tell each other anything.

"Jan, put your pride aside. No one wants to read about a smelly, hairy old dog." Jan is writing a book about his dog, assuming that the whole world will love him as much as he does.

"Hey, little hussy, how about you keep your opinions to yourself?"

Correction: Jan can tell *me* anything.

We're at the gate getting ready to "pre-board." *Pre-boarding? What does that even mean? Standing very close together in a holding room instead of sitting in the waiting area? Mentally preparing ourselves for the transition to Spanish culture? What does one do before boarding a plane?*

Pre-boarding is not standard. It is only done in exceptional circumstances. But with this low-cost airline, it happens on every flight. We're packed in with all the other passengers. I begin to wonder why I'm doing this. *Where is the fun?* Packing, repacking, checking in, queues, boarding—but only after pre-boarding—customs, unpacking ... and I have no idea what I'll be having for breakfast tomorrow. Or where I'll have it. There was a time when I loved this game. Not so much anymore. I even worry a bit about all the germs around me.

WEDNESDAY, DECEMBER 14

"Jan, who's better in purple, Bebé or Uma?"

"Depends. Do you want to bring home a young toreador, or a soccer-team owner in pinstripes?"

Jan and I adjust quickly to the Spanish rhythm and head out around ten in the evening for a glass of wine and a bite to eat. I remove Uma's auburn locks from my head and switch them for Bebé's long blonde hair.

"Russian blonde and shiny purple, I don't know. It screams soccer exec to me," says Jan teasingly.

"It's chic," I mutter as I smooth down my top. Some combinations just don't work, however hard I try. Like Platina's electric-white bob with a black and white print. Or Bebé's blonde locks with the thin straps of my pink minidress. It would send the wrong message. I like flashing my bimbo side every once in a while, but I keep it tempered at all times. I focus more on each character's best assets. Pam offers me all sorts of wardrobe possibilities, but now that I have nine characters to choose from, my options are endless. Which is why a green top for Uma and Sue is on my shopping list—to give their red locks a bit more oomph. Also on my list: a pink floral shirt to give Daisy a little extra sweetness, and a sexy black blouse to flaunt Bebé.

When I go out on the town, I always go for sexy and sultry—for obvious reasons: with a full mane of long, shiny hair, I'm halfway there. That's why Bebé, Uma, and Pam have seen the most restaurants, clubs, and parties. Tonight is no exception: red wine on Las Ramblas. And because Bebé, Sue, Pam, and Uma are the only ladies who've traveled with me to Barcelona, my choice is limited to blonde or red, purple or pink.

"Is it too much?" I ask.

"Too much for Bebé? I doubt it."

"Then this is it."

Roebelina Sletta Mongolia is my name tonight. Jan likes to rechristen me according to my outfit.

In the little restaurant where we end up, we order more plates than we can finish. Jan tells me about his life as he was growing up. About his first big love, going to Studio 54 in New York, meeting Andy Warhol, chasing Oprah in her own studio, the day that he became a millionaire (this lasted only a few days, until the next business transaction was done), and the early days of his TV show. He has had such a life. His big mouth brought him everywhere. And all I really know about his life is that he loves chocolates (preferably the ones from *Forrest Gump*), that he walks around with a little jar in the inside pocket of his jacket to spice up his coffee, and how he likes his eggs.

"You know, doll face, if you keep flirting on TV like you did last week ..."

"Then what?"

"Nothing, nothing, I'm not saying anything. We'll see."

THURSDAY, DECEMBER 15

I walk to the corner at the back of the church and pick out the three largest candles I can find. Next I find an empty spot to place the candles. This feels more respectful than jamming them between other prayers. Two saints watch over my candles, guarding them—I don't have a clue which ones, but they look very pious and responsible. I glance around the church. The huge chandeliers hanging from the ceiling make the space appear even larger.

Sitting in the first pew, I'm alone, with a mass of empty pews behind me. Jan's outside, with his face turned toward the sun. I'm tired, really tired. I can feel my head spinning. I don't know how many churches I have visited in my life. When Sis and I were little, our parents dragged us to every church in town, and since we were always road tripping, we have seen quite a few of them. It didn't convert any of us though. My father came to admire the architecture, my mom the shrine. And after vising the churches, my sister and I were promised an afternoon of our choice.

But since my chemo I have started coming to churches myself. I embrace the silence, the calm, and the fact that I'm always welcome—no matter what I said or did the day before. Safe behind these friendly walls, away from where everything moves so fast. I get up, lighting the candles. The first is for Mom, whose illness sort of got buried under mine, and although she functions well, she is still fighting the fear that the cancer might come back. The second is for Jur, and the third is for my new friend, Chantal. For some reason, I'm very excited about meeting her. I leave it at that, otherwise I could carry on forever, so many angels around me.

Two wrinkly old Spanish women shuffle by. Their steps slow as they approach the altar to light their candles, and our gazes meet. One of them flashes me a smile with no more than three remaining teeth, while the other busies herself putting coins into the narrow slot of the large jar beneath the altar. They have their moment, and I have mine, before they disappear back through the heavy wooden doors.

I sit down in the first row again, leaning back and looking straight into the eyes of Jesus, my now-familiar friend. Two eyes gazing down on me from above, always and everywhere. For the first time, it strikes me as a very comforting thought. Always and everywhere. I decide to light a fourth candle, for him. It's the least I can do.

FRIDAY, DECEMBER 16

There's something special about this church. I've come back every day. Hundreds of candles crowd every corner of the otherwise empty space. The ceiling vaults are high, the stone floor bare, and the pews empty. There isn't much grandeur, but it is a beautiful church.

Today two more old people shuffle by me. This time it's a couple, supporting each other with knees and elbows. They glance at me and greet me with a nod. Perhaps in the church my long blonde hair is associated more with an angel than a bimbo. Not like on Las Ramblas. I nod back and watch their path through the church, until it's quiet once again. I get up and walk to the exit, away from the burning candles. Away from the warmth of my friend. I look back one last time, to a space full of thoughts and prayers, and disappear through the large, imposing doors into the light where Jan's lean posture is waiting for me. I take his hand and we run down the stairs, laughing.

SATURDAY, DECEMBER 17

I walk into the church to check on my candles. They've burned out.

WEDNESDAY, DECEMBER 21

I'm back in Amsterdam and meeting Chantal at her favorite bar. It's still early and quiet. We sit together at one of the empty tables set up with glasses, ashtrays, and lit candles.

Chantal lights her second cigarette. She laughs cheerfully and takes another sip of her white wine. Opposite me sits a winner. An optimist. An exception to the rule. A woman who looked her greatest fear in the eye and dared to face it. She's still shining. She's made me laugh, sigh, listen closely, and swallow my tears. She gives me goose bumps because I can't let go of the thought that the chair opposite me could soon be empty.

Terminally ill. Enjoying life. Making jokes. Flirting. Shoe shopping. That was the first thing Chantal did when she was diagnosed: she bought new shoes, not caring how long she would have to walk in them, probably hoping they would lead her to a new life. Shivers run down my spine. I want to fold her in my arms. Not out of pity or sympathy, but to feel her strength.

Sitting here with her makes me sad. Sad about cancer. Sad about those jerks who can't handle cancer but "want to be friends." About assholes who choose young bodies without tumors or wigs over ours. Who would rather hold hands with a wrist not wearing a yellow rubber bracelet.

"Hate to break it to you, but these don't work," Chantal says with a wink as she shows me her bracelet.

She tells me the past tense is something she is afraid of. That her friends will talk about her in the past tense. That they will grow old and gray without her. I know what she means. Even though things are looking brighter for me now, I still don't dare to believe that time is on my side.

Am I terminally ill as well? Chantal's friend asks me this when she joins our party. The bar has grown crowded.

I shake my head, feeling relieved and slightly guilty.

Chantal, my new hero, jokes that she isn't planning on going anywhere anytime soon; she only just moved into her new place, after all.

"But I won't make forty," she says. Although we share the same sense of humor, my smile feels forced.

She says Sunday is the worst day of the week, because that's the day you're supposed to spend with your loved ones and she's all alone. I imagine her standing behind a window looking down at the people on the streets, walking and living. I suddenly feel lucky to still live with my parents. I think about how I could cheer her up. Maybe we could spend our Sundays whining together. Or have fun buying shoes together without wondering how often we'll get to wear them. The doctors have given her two years. She reckons more than that. So do I.

There's a lot we've had to give up, but we have a lot left, too. We have every second, minute, and hour of the day for ourselves. We have every day of the week for ourselves. We live for ourselves and for those we love.

TUESDAY, DECEMBER 27

I climb into my hot bath, no candles and no lover. I leaf through *Elle* and my eye falls on the horoscope, which I usually cut out for Annabel, but now—against my better judgment—decide to read. The mysteries of the stars and the solar system condensed into seven hundred words per astrological sign, divided into character analysis, career nonsense, and unrealistic love-life predictions.

As far as work goes, I'll run into some bad luck in September. That's too bad as I'm planning on launching my writing career just in that month. *NL20* has offered me a permanent position, and the feedback of the editor who I met at the TV studio was super positive. He read the diary I kept all this time in the hospital and he wants to publish it as a book! Why not dream big, now that my ability to dream has been given back to me?

In terms of love, the road ahead is looking pretty bumpy. *Great. I haven't even gotten over the last one.* Apparently I will meet two princes this year: the first will screw me over before the summer, leaving me to be someone else's prince. All bets on the second, then, who will turn up at my doorstep in the fall. According to my horoscope, that one's a keeper. *Can I trust the stars? Can I finally stop thinking about Jur, then?*

THURSDAY, DECEMBER 29

As Platina I sit on the terrace of Café Finch, writing, a blond man sits down at the table next to me. I have been discreetly studying him: *Cute, no doubt about that.* With plenty of hair too.

"Young lady, is that white hair all your own?" he asks.

I smile. "No, sir, that white hair comes right off."

"Oh. Is there a nasty reason for that which you'd rather not discuss?"

"Yes," I say.

"Oh. Is that why you're drinking mint tea rather than wine?"

"Yes."

"Do you mind me being so bold as to come sit next to you and ask you some more of these impertinent questions?"

"No, I quite like it."

"Good. Then, before we start, would you like another cup of tea?"

"I would like that very much."

"Lady!" he shouts over the terrace. "Can I have two fresh mint teas, please?" He comes and sits next to me. The terrace is small and cramped, even on a sunny winter day like today, but he finds a way not to sit too close to me.

"My name is Allard and I'm very happy to meet you. I must admit, I have seen you here before, looking slightly different." His act makes me laugh.

"My name is Platina and we'll see about that."

"In that case, we have to converse a little longer. I mean, to be able to know. Are you sure I'm not disturbing you in your ... Were you writing?"

"Just taking some notes."

"Interesting. What are you taking notes of?"

He doesn't stop asking me questions, and I love it, all this curiosity from an attractive man who makes me laugh every other minute and who doesn't seem to be afraid of me wearing a wig.

"Everything."

"That's quite a lot."

"It is."

FRIDAY, DECEMBER 30

Chantal is sitting beside me while I do one of my last chemos. It's just like in *Sex and the City* in the episode where they eat popsicles around Samantha while she does her chemo. Only we're eating ladyfingers.

Ten minutes after I got started she walked in, and now, an hour and a half later, she's still here. I think we've really found each other, whether we're sharing a bottle of wine or a bag of chemo. We can see the fun in all of it. Chantal prefers to take care of all hospital business alone, without emotions. Her family lives in France, so there's not as much pressure. She is due to have a scan next week, she tells me. I ask her if anyone is coming along.

"You?" she asks happily.

"Definitely."

Yes, we have cancer and that sucks, but life goes on. Even for Chantal, who six months ago was given the news that her treatment would become a prolongation instead of a cure. I ask her if she has thought about her funeral yet.

"Cremation."

Rotting away beneath the ground doesn't appeal to her.

"How about you?" she asks me.

"Burial. I'm thinking about those you leave behind. I can imagine wanting to be burned and thrown into the wind, but my family wouldn't know where I was. Have you picked anything out?"

"An urn? No, not yet. Why don't you take care of it? Then I'll do yours, if that's how it turns out."

We laugh at the thought of me orchestrating her big day and she doing mine. We want the same kind of thing, except she wants DJ Tiësto and I want the Rolling Stones.

"It has to be a great party," she says.

Chantal and I discuss coffins just as easily as her latest shoe purchase or book experience. And when it comes to men, we tell each other everything. We both know how it feels to desperately want to go home with a guy—no baggage, no strings attached—after spending three days throwing up in bed or coming straight off an IV drip.

"Cancer bitches," Chantal calls us. A cancer bitch still ends up at random parties and wakes up in the morning with a killer hangover. "Those hangovers are so much worse now," she says.

I've left most of that behind me. Regular hangovers are not part of my lifestyle anymore. These days I meditate, go to therapy, and try anything that might help keep the cancer at bay. Because I want to. I don't want to pretend the danger isn't there. But if any of us were given the choice, you'd pick my prognosis over hers. And that's why Chantal crams in all the parties she can.

"Rest in peace," she calls as she leaves to do her grocery shopping.

"Have a nice funeral," I call after her.

Chantal gives me the same comfort as Marco and Oscar when I think about dying, which doesn't go much further than blackness, or maybe an energy field here and there. The chances that I go before her are slim to none, however bubbly and healthy she appears now. It's a very selfish thought, I know, but it feels nice to know that I'll have a real friend up there in the blackness before one day I go.

Damn. How lonely she must be.

SUNDAY, JANUARY 1

The New Year has begun. I think all this "new year, new you" reflection is a little over the top, but all around me people are saying how much 2005 SUCKED and how GREAT 2006 is going to be. All this with meaningful looks and hugs.

I don't say it out loud, but I think today SUCKS. The city is deserted. I hate New Year's, always have. And I'm out of yogurt.

What has changed since last year? My prognosis, obviously, which is better than GREAT. My sister living in Hong Kong with her now fiancé: SUCKS. Chantal in my life: GREAT. Her prognosis: SUCKS. *NL20*: GREAT. Love life? DOUBLE SUCKS.

WEDNESDAY, JANUARY 4

Dr. N hangs up the photos from my last scan and contemplates the results with a smile on his face. I think I detect some pride in his expression as well. Also on his screem my lung appears to be clean.

He listens patiently to my lungs with his stethoscope. This man is clearly passionate about his work. I sigh and cough and he says everything sounds clear.

"But this is fantastic! he exclaims in a typical Professor Calculus manner. And this time he isn't afraid to give me an optimistic prognosis—not the case with Dr. L—by telling me that, in his opinion, my tumor and its entire family are gone. You can never be completely sure, he reminds me. But it's good enough for me.

Now I have to wean my body off the meds. From ten milligrams to five milligrams of prednisone. I make an appointment with the local physiotherapist to get my muscles and stamina back up to scratch. Three gym sessions and only two chemos to go. One more scan and then I'm free until the summer. The summer! That means six months without Dr. N, and soon Dr. L and my nurses. The thought scares me a bit. Weird how you can get used to anything. Even cancer.

THURSDAY, JANUARY 5

On my way to see Dr. K, caught up in the excitement, I almost forget to bring along my last CT scan images.

My heart is beating fast. It's pumping warm blood throughout my chest, all the way down to my stomach. Thick, healthy blood is being pumped around my body, leaving a pink trace on my cheeks. Tingling in my fingertips. A slight tremor in my legs. No shallow breaths but audible gulps of fresh air.

Dr. K looks at me for a long time. This time he doesn't settle for a handshake but pulls me close. He kisses me on both cheeks. Am I imagining it, or is there some old-fashioned flirting going on here? I quickly run down the list of compliments he's given me in the past fifteen minutes.

A few months have passed since I shared a space alone with him. There has been ample reason to keep in touch via e-mail, though, which I have fully optimized. The content of those e-mails has shifted somewhat over the months from purely medical to private matters. Up until last month we didn't get much further than discussing pneumonitis or an endoscope; now he broaches the subject of the media attention and my fledgling writing career. And where I started with "Dr. K" and "Regards, Sophie," I now happily type in "Dear K" and "X Sophie."

The telephone rings. An unexpected bellowing laugh, which makes me smile. After hanging up, he smoothly switches back to lung content and fibrosis. And there it is again, that look. Eye contact lasting a few long seconds, enough to make the nerves beneath my skin glow. Was he seeing himself kissing me passionately on his examination bench? Or is this wishful thinking only on my side of the desk?

I leave his office with a smile on my face. My phone is beeping. Rob thinks I'm a "fantastic chick," loves me very much, and hopes to love me for a long time to come. Does he hope that when he's lying on top of her? *Bugger off.*

My phone beeps again. It's Jur, asking if I'm okay. *I'm great, my dear friend*. I dream of a guy who thinks of me as just a friend and get flustered by a doctor I have an impossible crush on. When will love ever get simple?

FRIDAY, JANUARY 13

This morning I was walking down the street softly singing along to James Blunt's voice in my ear. A boy carrying a skateboard in one hand and an enormous bag with something orange sticking out of it—a pumpkin?—in the other was walking beside me. He asked me about the time and started talking to me about his parties at Club 11, where he works. So that's where I'm going tonight for *NL20*, for my next column. I'm a party journalist now; I better keep my ears open.

I take the elevator in the old post office building on the wharf all the way up to the eleventh floor. Pumpkin Boy is standing next to me, but he doesn't recognize me. After all, I was Pam yesterday, and today I'm Uma. I thought Uma would fit in better at the party. I look him straight in the eye but say nothing. I take my time, thoroughly checking him out. I decide to leave it at that.

Upstairs I go in search of good people to photograph for the article. I'm here to work, after all, and have five hundred words to fill. Usually it's a challenge to find enough interesting people, and I'm happy if I come across one remotely funky guy with an earring, maybe even a leather jacket, but tonight my camera's memory card can hardly handle the load.

"Love the lashes, I have the same ones," a transsexual blonde tells me. Wow, that's a new one. I should come here more often.

"Thanks," I reply as I move on through the crowd.

I get a kiss from a boy in a mask; his T-shirt says STICKER SLUT. Two piercing-covered lesbians wearing black makeup and fiery-red lipstick shimmy by. They're perfect candidates for a picture and I skip after them.

Suddenly I spot Tie Boy, grooving away in his All Stars. I tap him on the shoulder. "Tie Boy!"

He turns around and recognizes me immediately. Now that I've written about him in *NL20*, he knows all about my wigs. He grabs me around the waist and plants a long kiss on my cheek. "And who is gracing me with her presence this evening?"

"Uma."

"Uma suits you. Drink?"

At the bar he orders vodka for himself and a mineral water for me.

"Can I feel?" he asks as he points at my hair.

"Sure, go ahead."

"Fake, all right. So, would you like to go out sometime?"

I smile and nod.

After taking endless photos of beautiful, interesting people, I put away my camera and go in search of the manager, whom I'm supposed to meet. I'm shown to a room at the back of the club. I find him surrounded by pretty women, standing behind a table, cigarette in hand, with a bottle of rum. It's a short conversation; he's far more interested in the rum and the women.

On my way out I run into Allard on the dance floor. He gives me a big kiss—it seems as though everyone is in the same building tonight. I love nights out where you keep running into familiar faces. Allard and I run down the eleven flights of stairs together because the elevator has broken down. He thinks I'm pretty and exciting but is too afraid to flirt with me, worried he'll scare me off. I know he means well, but it also annoys the hell out of me. As if getting sick means I can't handle a little harmless flirting. On top of that: flirting is the best there is!

"Allard?"

"Yes?"

"Remember that day on the terrace at Finch, when we first met? Were you drunk then?"

"Drunk? Tipsy at most, why?"

"When you told me you thought I was beautiful?"

"Yes."

"Is that still the case or was it the white wig you fancied?"

He laughs. "As far as hair goes, I think you've only improved."

"So you like me even more?"

"What are you getting at?"

"How come I've only seen you twice since then?"

"I assumed you had a boyfriend."

"What if I told you I was single?"

"Then what?" He looks like he's starting to catch on.

"Then would you take me out to dinner?"

"Would you like that?"

I give him a seductive look. "Purely hypothetical."

"Perhaps."

"Does it have anything to do with the reason why I'm wearing a wig?"

"Sophie?"

"Just answer the question."

"Okay … I would be lying if I said that didn't scare me. But it has nothing to do with the fact that I haven't asked you out. I just want to be careful with you. Something about you makes me careful, that's all."

"Okay."

"What is it you want?"

"I want you to kiss me as if I'm just a girl."

And he does.

When I get back home my phone beeps; it's Pumpkin Boy asking why he didn't see me at the party.

I look at the photos I took. They are a flurry of polka-dot scarves, striped sweaters, and tiger-print pantyhose. Allard, the fierce lesbians, Pumpkin Boy with Uma, and more all flash by me with the club in the background.

Before I fall asleep I check my e-mail. Chantal has written again. She says she's been extremely tired, sleeping more than twelve hours a night. She ends the e-mail saying that she will pop by my chemo next week. We made a point of knowing each other's schedules.

FRIDAY, JANUARY 20

"So," Esther says, pricking into my synthetic boob for the last time. "Who is this Dr. K, anyway?"

I spill my secret crush to her with a grin on my face.

"I thought so!" she exclaims. "When you were on TV you got to kiss my two favorite men in life, you know. What's that actor like in real life? He seems like he'd be such a genuine guy. And then the host, Matthijs, of course—what a hunk."

For a moment I feel bad for my nurse—here I am, fishing in her pond—but I don't feel bad for long: that's just my gray cloud's silver lining.

FRIDAY, JANUARY 27

I'm tagging along with Chan to her chemo for the first time. The morgue is on the same floor as the parking garage at Chantal's hospital. There's no way to avoid it after parking the car. *How morbid.*

"Scary, huh? That I'll be down here someday?"

It sure is. With that in mind we walk down the hall toward radiology. My mood is sour. Imagine what Chantal must be feeling.

"Chan are you scared of dying?"

"Very. Try not to think about it."

"Yeah."

"It's more a feeling. A constant feeling of panic."

Still, she's amazingly relaxed. As if she's made peace with her terminal verdict. As long as I haven't been given that verdict, every new scan and test turns me into a bundle of nerves. Maybe that's because she has been given the final verdict already.

But we're not playing deaf. For all the securities that have been taken away from us, we have been given the greatest security of all in return, a second chance at *really* living our lives. On the Internet, there are so many people proclaiming how they feel happier and more complete as a cancer patient. Big words. I recognize some of that in myself and in Chantal, too, but it doesn't make the island we're stuck on much more fun.

Back home I change wigs and inspect my eyes in the mirror. My eyelashes have grown a few millimeters this week. I stick on my longest fake lashes with gold glitter and opt for Daisy. Her look is so fearless that I can't help but feel as confident as she looks. That should make an impression.

Sitting at Finch, I bat my lashes to get the attention of my favorite bartender. He joins me at the end of the bar and puts his arms around my shoulders.

"Mint tea?" he asks.

"Yes, please." As Bartender moves his arm he accidentally takes Daisy along with him. My wig is hanging halfway down my back, revealing my baby hairs and bald spots. I blush. Bartender helps me to quickly get my wig back in place. We both move on with our drinks. I go back to my seat. I feel as if I've just been caught while putting something in my handbag that isn't mine. (This sometimes happens; I have a weak spot for espresso cups with a personalized restaurant logo on it.) When I walk out the café thirty minutes later I'm still blushing.

FRIDAY, FEBRUARY 10

Today I crossed out the fifty-fourth week in my agenda. After this I am officially done. It takes me forty minutes to get to the hospital. I'm alone. No Mom, no Oma, no Sis, no Chantal. I've brought some chocolate to give to Dr. L. The shops are full of hearts; it's almost Valentine's Day. I immediately thought about buying something heart-shaped for Dr. K, but I think I've annoyed his wife enough. And Dr. L wouldn't get the joke. No hearts this year, to give or receive.

Nurse Pauke hooks me up. Today I'm her assistant. I get to hold the needle and unscrew the pink casing. I mess it up immediately; I've already squirted the contents all over myself before she can get it into my port-a-cath. Not as easy as it looks, being a nurse.

Later on I take a walk downstairs with my IV. I don't like it here: people look at me. Whether it's my IV pole, my synthetic boob or my wig, I attract their attention and it's not wanted.

I chat a little with my neighbor about hair loss and hair growth, and we end our conversation by saying we hope never to see each other again. That's probably the nicest and most common sentence uttered at the outpatient clinic.

Dr. L accepts my chocolates with a warm smile. Not only is his desk a mess, but the floor is covered in exploding dossiers, piled high into crooked towers. He apologizes for the chaos and gives me, as always, a firm handshake. We discuss my blood values and my next appointment. The atmosphere is different. I'm not here because I hope he will cure me. I'm here because I hope I am cured and will never have to come back here again. My blood values are on the rise, my next appointments purely routine. I happily tell him how much better I'm feeling. That I've gained some weight and can feel my energy coming back. That I know for sure that the cancer is gone.

"So my port-a-cath can be taken out already? Shouldn't I leave it in for a while just to be sure?"

Dr. L shakes his head. "You're better now, aren't you? You're done."

We're quiet for a minute but then raise our heads to speak at the exact same time. His eyes are flashing with thoughts, as are mine. So many moments of uncertanties and awkwardness behind us. So many consults and handshakes to get us to this point.

He says what I'm afraid to say: "I'll miss you."

I leave the room with a lump in my throat. I actually think I've come to really like him.

* * *

After being unhooked from the IV, I feel fine. Outside I take the tram instead of a taxi. On the way home I stop for some books and a coffee. I've wanted to read Ray Kluun's book, *Love Life*, ever since Chantal assured me it's more drama than sensation. Kluun has written the best cancer book ever, about losing his wife to cancer and how he loses himself in affairs and partying as a way to cope. It doesn't sound very loving but it actually is a beautiful love story. There are two shoes on the book cover. Women's sneakers. I don't know why, but

I'm sure I'll find out. With Kluun under my arm I walk into Finch. It's almost five, the Noordermarkt is filling up, and I happily observe the hustle and bustle around me. It all looks and sounds so different to me now that my last chemo is over.

Sitting in the café until closing time, clothes smelling of smoke and beer. Getting dragged out of bed in the morning to go to Pilates with Annabel. Partying till late. Gossiping about guys.

I'm back.

MONDAY, FEBRUARY 13

Now that my fifty-fourth week is over and the last hand has been shaken with Dr. L, I'm no longer a patient. Today I am a "writer." It sounds kind of poshy and I'd say it suits me better than studying economics on a blackboard anyway.

I'm starting to fit the writing picture. My laptop and I are adjusting quite nicely. I get up in the morning and write a little. I have breakfast and come up with some ideas. Go to bed and write some more. The words just keep on coming. I write all day long. It somehow seems meant to be.

THURSDAY, FEBRUARY 16

It's snowing; the snowflakes shimmer past my large windows a thousand at a time. Dressed in a black dress and very sheer pantyhose, which will be more laddered than solid black after one wear, I climb into an unfamiliar car. Disco glitter and party wigs. The occasion is the launch of a new party boat in an industrial part of Amsterdam—a good reason to go reporting. And it's a wig-themed party, an even better reason for me to write about it. My date, Tie Boy, is wearing a velvet pinstripe suit for the occasion. My long blonde hair hardly makes an impression tonight; all the crazy hairstyle creations surrounding me are an inspiration, and wigs are handed around laughingly. Pink curls, white flowing locks, a black Afro.

Onstage, among all the sweating partygoers, Tie Boy comes and stands close behind me. My body is covered in the dress's thin elastic material, pulled tightly over my hips. Bebé's hair is dancing wildly around my head and my lips sing to the music. I feel free, especially knowing Rob doesn't make up any part of Bebé's existence. Tie Boy's hand slowly slides down my back and then pulls away again. This happens a few times, until I turn around and look him straight in his big, blue eyes. This is our moment. He tightens his grip; his hand is low around my middle and moves playfully toward my belly button. One touch and I have goose bumps all over. One more touch and I'm filled with irresistible desire. We look at each other and want one thing. His warm hand slips into mine and we disappear. Away from the stage, away from the sweating partygoers. I started the evening as Bebé, but I finish the night as Cicciolina, a white-blonde wig with more sex than style, given to me as a souvenir.

"Want to come up for a nightcap?" he asks. It's one A.M.

"Will you make me a cup of tea?" I ask him, happy that I don't have to say good-bye to him just yet. We climb a long, steep stairway—me doing my best not to trip in my high heels—and pass a darkly painted bathroom, bedroom, and kitchen. I make a pit stop to adjust my unfamiliar hair.

"I only have rose hip." Tie Boy is obviously not a tea drinker. As we wait for the water to boil, meaningful glances bounce back and forth through the kitchen. And then his lips are on my temple, my cheekbone, carefully moving down toward my mouth. After hours of built-up tension our lips have found each other and don't let go. I want more—more of his lips, his hands, and especially his arms. We disappear into the room next door.

His lips slowly move lower. His fingers slip carefully inside. My mouth makes heaving noises, my back curls up. We're making love and I want to completely let go but I can't.

I see white coats, needles, Dr. L, then Rob. A tear runs down my cheek, down my arm. I think about Rob and what I saw in his eyes. *I don't see that right now.*

I think about how I got here. I want to let go, leave it all behind me, and make room for new things and people, but I can't. I feel trapped in my own story.

Crying softly I fall asleep, and crying softly I wake up. It's dark, and I blink a few times before I can make out the contours of the room. A feeling of loneliness creeps up on me.

I'm on my right side, with my back to the other body in the bed with me; only our feet are touching. I turn around and creep up against the warm, sleeping body, wanting to cuddle away the sudden emptiness in me. But the closer I try to get, the further away I feel from myself.

FRIDAY, FEBRUARY 17

In the morning I meet Jan for a coffee. Can he see that I cried? That this morning, when the city was still dark and sleeping, I washed off my sadness in the shower?

Probably not. How can he possibly see all that, when even I forget it by the time I wake up? So much goes unnoticed. Not just by those around me, but also by myself.

Here they are again. The unexpected moods. The sudden tears. The spontaneous sobs. I slice an onion and start to cry, a few stinging tears growing into a waterfall. First they roll down my cheeks. I catch them with my lips and lick them clean with my tongue. *Salty.* I keep chopping away on the cutting board to the rhythm of my breathing, trying to calm myself down. No easy task. The path from prognosis and consultations in the hospital to carefree glasses of wine and wig-themed parties is a long one. I run away from my fearful tears into the night.

THURSDAY, FEBRUARY 23

"I mean, obviously I'm worried about your health. Are they absolutely sure you'll get better? And all the chemo doesn't do much for me physically. Slipping wigs, contraptions in your chest, all that stuff—they aren't exactly my fetishes. Sorry, I just don't think it's going to work out."

"Yeah, definitely not," I say, hanging up the phone. It's clear: dating is not for girls with wigs. I'm stunned. *Is that really what he thinks? Did he really dump me because I wear a wig?* So much for Tie Boy and Platina. *Wow, this hurts.*

"A girl with cancer has to work harder for a bit of attention than a girl without, that's just the way it is!" These conversations are usually held in the pub, me holding a warm cup of tea and my friends exhaling their cigarette smoke and raising beers to their lips. It's ridiculous. As if I have some sort of handicap.

Even though it's not the same as it was, I still flirt. I still use all the same tricks: knees touching under the table, coy smiles. The only difference now is that I already know I won't be going home with that person. Not tonight, or tomorrow night either. It just doesn't feel right. A lot has to happen before the first drink turns into the first sleepover these days.

Nowadays when men look at me it means one of three things: either they see something they like, they see a booger hanging from my nose, or they see that something is not quite right. I'm most afraid of that last one. It makes me feel so aware of my wig and the bare head hiding underneath. Or worried there might be some unexpected dark fuzz sticking out from under my blonde curls.

I'm aware of the statement I make when I walk in with one of my wild wigs. But the attention also makes me uncomfortable. The TV host called my story "a life with a secret" when he interviewed me. He was intrigued by this girl who left her cancer behind as she stepped out into the city night in her best pumps. The girl who lets a stranger kiss her without revealing anything of her true reality.

But that same girl goes to the market in the morning. I see people looking at me; some even tell me they love my hair. From a distance it's all great, but seeing the fright in the saleslady's eyes when I come out of the fitting room and my wig is hanging down the back of my dress is less fun. It jerks me back to that nasty place where my disease scares people off. But that same disease has become such a huge part of who I am.

I see men looking at Bebé's or Pam's sexy blonde locks, and I see them thinking about things I would rather not be a part of. I can't help wondering if they would be thinking the same things if it were Sue or Stella sipping green tea here at the bar. Or just me, brown fuzz on display. They don't know me bald. Bald in my bed, bald in the shower, bald in my white dressing gown, bald when my wig slips off as I pull my sweater over my head. What would they say to that? There's so much they don't know about me.

I live in a different world. That's my secret. And I keep it that way, because I don't like to talk about my reality. If I could just say 'yeah I have cancer and you what do you do?' I would but it doesn't work that way. I better hide it. It saves me a lot of disbelieving and scared looks.

Let them think I'm a blonde bimbo who paints her toenails scarlet red. That I'm a carefree redhead drinking mojitos. A studious political scientist, as I sit in the library amid books with my hair pulled back. Let them think that's who I am. It's all partly true, but really, I'm just a girl looking for love.

TUESDAY, MAY 2

"Sophie! Sophie!" An annoying nurse is shouting in my ear.

I open my eyes. Mom is sitting next to me. *Wow, I was really out of it.* Quite pleasant, that anesthetic. I hold my gaze on my mother until she comes back into focus. Suddenly I see her as she was two years ago. Her hair is gathered up into a messy bun, like it was then. She seems younger, less worried, and more herself. She's beautiful.

"How are you feeling?" asks the nurse.

"Like I want to sleep some more."

"That's fine. No pain?"

"No." I push myself upright and look for my bump. No more bump. Welcome to my body, strange dent. "Where did it go?"

The nurse brings out my port-a-cath. I've never seen it before. It looks different than I had imagined; plastic and white, not as sci-fi as I had imagined. I could have gotten it removed a little earlier but didn't feel any rush. Too sentimental.

"Can I keep it?"

THURSDAY, MAY 4

"I'm sorry, girls, but this just won't be enough. You need about a kilo per person; you lose quite a lot after peeling."

Annabel looks at the twenty white asparagus in her hand. Well, that's that. The scale shows exactly 1.3 kilos, and according to her mother, Eva, that's 700 grams short.

The asparagus are in season again. And this year I can comb my hair. It's dark and about two inches long, with a bit of a curl.

Annabel and I walk out, back to the vegetable grocer.

FRIDAY, MAY 5

Sis has come to see us for a few weeks. She strokes my arm with her soft fingertips, down to my wrist and then back up. She holds still at my scar. We're lying so close together that our foreheads touch. So close that Hong Kong feels only a wink away.

She tells me about the beautiful islands of the city where she now lives, about how they house so many people in such little space, how she feels the skyscraper she lives in moving when the weather is stormy. She tells me about the job she found and her bitchy boss, about a friend who won a marathon in the Gobi Desert, about delicious fried eggplant swimming around in a big bowl at a Chinese restaurant, about a market called the wet market and the horrible way turtles are treated, about how the Chinese are so much smaller than she is but still always seem to block her way. About hiking in the New Territories, how I can't imagine the beauty, hours of jungle and then a clear blue bay to dive into at the end of the trail. About a Chinese girl named Lucienne who she met at a dinner party and who I should meet.

She looks and sounds so grown-up. Living a grown-up life with her boyfriend in a faraway city, wearing elegant suits and heels. Her life sounds like a dream to me. And it confuses me. What am I doing here when the world is out there? But which world? Hadn't I just decided that my world is here, in between my loved ones?

Whatever it is, I can't wait to go and see it all myself.

FRIDAY, MAY 12

PINK RIBBON it says on the bracelet I've just slipped over my wrist. In the bookstore we pass a pile of books on the way to the thrillers and bestsellers. *Help, My Wife Is Pregnant!* I read.

"That's supposed to be good, too, but I don't particularly want to read it." Chantal walks straight on to another pile of books, one without pregnancies, ovarian tubes, or bibs. She must feel so lonely in a room like this with so many stories. Stories about falling in love, getting married, having babies, growing old. For her this is all past tense.

We have a drink on the terrace of the Café Pilsvogel. As I pluck at my pink bracelet I realize I'm missing my yellow one. Lost yet another. Yellow stands for a lot: Marco, Salvatore, and Lance. Pink is for Chantal, trapped in a body full of cancer. I won't lose this one; I made sure to get the smallest size.

Chan is drinking wine; I'm having tea. Chan has a great tan and beside her I look almost see-through. But she's riddled with cancer and I'm clean. As I work through the foodplatter in front of us, Chantal tells me she's been having a hard time seeing the point lately. Her cynical tone permeates everything she says, whether it's about foodplatters, doctors, or love.

"Nothing is fun anymore. I don't know what's wrong, but when I wake up all I want to do is go right back to sleep. Everyone thinks I'm having a great time because I spend every day sitting in bars laughing and joking around, but I'm only there because, really, I'm all alone."

I take another bite.

"In ten years' time—if I make it that far—I won't be able to use my arm, the doctors told me. From the radiation."

"Oh, well, luckily you won't be around by then," I say.

"Sure you won't have a glass of wine?" she asks.

"No, thanks."

"You know, I've been having the worst headaches lately. Sometimes they keep me up at night."

"Are you worried?"

She shrugs. "I don't know. A few weird things happened this week."

"Like what?"

"My friend Ellen came around last night, and when I went to open the door to let her in, I forgot how to turn the key. The same thing happened on the toilet. I forgot how to flush."

"That could get dirty."

Chantal doesn't laugh. Neither do I. "Have you gone to see your doctor yet?"

"She's on vacation."

"So what, she has colleagues, doesn't she?"

"Yes, she does. But I'm seeing her on Thursday, I'll just ask her then."

"Chan, that's a week from now, why don't you go before then?"

"I'll see how it goes."

SATURDAY, MAY 13

It's evening and my phone rings. Chantal.

"Hey, honey, how is your headache doing?" I ask.

"Not good. It got really bad last night and I've been in the hospital all day. I rang Ellen and we drove over here straightaway. Waiting, waiting, you know how it is."

"And?"

"Nothing. They don't do any scans on Saturday, so I have to wait until Monday."

"They won't do an MRI?"

"I guess not."

"Do you want me to come over?"

"No, thanks, I'm completely exhausted. I'm going to take a shot of morphine and go to bed."

"All right. I'll call you tomorrow. Sleep well."

SUNDAY, MAY 14

I call Chantal in the afternoon. No answer. I call again. Still no answer. An hour later I call again and Ellen picks up. Something's wrong.

"Hi, Ellen, this is Sophie. How's Chan?"

Silence, hesitation. "Sophie, Chan isn't feeling so great, she'll call you back later on this week. Okay?"

That's a bad sign. "Shit. Can I come by?"

"Well, we're just leaving."

"To go to the hospital?"

"Yes."

"Shall I meet you there?"

"There's not much point. All she can do is vomit. She feels really bad."

"Shit."

"Why don't you take my number? You can always call me."

As I take down her digits I feel my first tears for Chan fall onto the piece of paper. For Chan, who is dying. Right now? In a few weeks? Months? Years? Complete helplessness. I've never felt that so strongly before. Now I'm the one sitting next to the bed. So much has changed again so fast. I decide to go to the hospital right away.

Within thirty minutes I arrive at the hospital, sweaty, puffing, in distress. In front of the entrance are two benches. I sit down on one of the benches and cry in silence. It's six thirty P.M. and the sun is shining, but I don't feel anything. I'm wearing my winter coat.

You would think that I would be used to all this by now. That I would know what she needs to hear and what she doesn't. But I have no clue. Should I even be here? Should I act cool or be more like Chan and make jokes?

At the foot of her bed, I watch how she slowly slips away, and I have no idea what to do. There's less and less of Chan, and more and more of cancer. Why is it that she's dying and I'm not? Is it just dumb luck? It bothers me that people who have no idea say that the right attitude will get you through. What would they say now?

MONDAY, MAY 15

Two things on the schedule for today: my scan at nine A.M. and then on to Chan's hospital, just to be with her, to make stupid jokes that don't make us laugh anymore.

As I slide under the machine I think about my prognosis and Chan's. "Wake up and smell the coffee"—that's what they call this feeling. That's how it feels to see your friend hanging over the toilet after you've been floating on air for a few months.

"Hey, look who it is!" In the hospital, Esther snaps shut the file she's working on and grabs mine, which is about a foot thick.

"Love your hair like this."

"Cool, right? All my own, with a little help from L'Oréal," I tell her. I decided to dye my short coupe blonde and to leave my wigs home, She asks after all the new gossip. I smile and give her the rundown of the latest developments in my life as a single girl and debuting author.

Dr. L approaches, but not to join in our conversation. He's here to check up on my body, not my hair. Like a real doctor, Dr. L isn't easily distracted.

"How do you feel?" he asks me.

"Good."

"No complaints? Stabbing pains, tingling?"

"No."

"Are you having your scan now?" Dr. L might make my appointments, but I keep track of them.

"No, just had it. So, I'll see you tomorrow?"

"Let's not put that off. I'll fit you in."

"Great."

"I like your hair like that."

"Thanks."

* * *

On my way to Chantal's room I pass by the morgue.

Scary, huh? That I'll be down here someday? Chantal's words still give me goose bumps. What idiotic architect planned this hospital, anyway?

In the chemo ward all the women have short hair, I fit in perfectly. There are some baldies and here and there a wig or a head scarf. Chantal has the thickest and longest hair of them all; cancer has a very good sense for irony. She's on the fourth floor, wing C, room 1. The card slipped into her door reads EMERGENCY.

She is lying in bed. Her friend Ellen sits next to her. I imagine the loneliness she must be feeling because she'll be the first to go. She punctuates my thoughts by puking up her breakfast.

"Show Sophie the magazine," she says to Ellen.

Her friend hands me a glossy magazine. "Page sixty-four," she says.

I turn the pages. A glowing Chantal, with the headline I HAVE TO LIVE THIS LIFE TO THE FULLEST. Chan and her life philosophy in the spotlights. Cancer really does sell.

Chantal Smithuis (34) is terminally ill. She is expected to die from breast cancer within two years. She wants to give a voice to all those women who don't make it. And to tell us how, to her own surprise, she is happier than ever.

I look past the magazine pages to the sick girl lying in bed, drugged up with morphine and dexamethasone. *Some happiness.* I speak to her in a soft voice. She answers in a slow, rasping whisper.

"This is what I was afraid of. Being admitted to *this* hospital." She's in the serious-cancer-patient hospital now. Although Chantal has been undergoing treatment at this hospital for a while, she has never been admitted overnight. "The beginning of the end," she mumbles.

I stay quiet, robbed of all my words. Ellen goes to get some fresh air. The room smells of chicken broth from the plastic cup that sits next to her hospital bed. She can't keep it down. A continuous cycle of swallowing, heaving, and vomiting. Bile and exhaust fumes from the helicopter flying around in her head for the past three days. Thank God she has a room to herself.

When the curtain opens we look up. A worried-looking face appears; wrinkled forehead, middle-aged. On his name tag is written a name and "neurologist". A nurse behind him. The neurologist shakes our hands one at a time. Then his hand moves to Chantal's shoulder, where it stays.

"It's not good news, I'm afraid. Metastases of the tumor have spread to your brain." Doctors really don't mince words around here. I swallow and look at Chan, the braver of the two of us.

She's pissed off. "Thirty-four," she says. "I'm fucking thirty-four." Her middle finger goes up. It's the first time I've seen her cry.

"We'll have to start you on radiation straightaway."

"And then what? Will that get rid of it?"

"It's worth a try."

"Will it make me go bald again?"

"Yes."

"How many metastases are we talking about?" she asks.

"They've spread all throughout the head."

"Shit. That's the third time it's come back. I can't believe how fast it comes. I was feeling so good these few months without chemo and now *bam!* It's in my head." She looks at me.

"Where's your notebook, Sophie? I thought you wanted to write a book about cancer." *Bam.*

I give Chan a kiss and tell her I'll be back soon. The tram is already waiting at the stop and I run as fast as I can. During the whole ride I look outside the window and cry, cry, cry.

TUESDAY, MAY 16

Rob sits with me in the waiting area. I'm happy that he's with me again. I follow the hands of the clock, watch the drawn faces of the people around me, wiggle back and forth on the uncomfortable plastic seat, and look at Rob. He squeezes my shoulder and gives me a kiss on my cheek. It doesn't take more than a few minutes before I see Dr. L approaching. He's smiling.

I sigh with relief. The thing is, the fear didn't leave my body together with the cancer. Now, without chemo, it's sort of probation time: is it really gone or will my body be full of swimming cancer cells again in a few months time? I wonder when the day will come that I don't worry about cancer anymore, but about something mundain as paying the rent.

"Miss van der Stap." Outside his office I'm still a "Miss." I get up, shake his hand, and will him to hold his smile. It works.

"Well, it all looks fine. Some minor changes from the last images, but in all probability those are effects from the radiation. How are you feeling?"

"Great. I feel great."

* * *

I go straight from the good news to the bad news: Chantal.

"How did your scan go?"

"Good," I say softly. It feels wrong to celebrate next to a head full of tumors. How do you tell someone who is dying that every day brings you closer to living again?

"Oh, good, I'm glad." She smiles. "At least one of us is clean."

MONDAY, MAY 19

I read the newspaper and shamefacedly have to admit that I have no idea what the political cartoon I'm reading is referring to. *Did I or did I not study political science? Where is my head at?*

Not in the newspapers, that's for sure. My head is somewhere else entirely. I'm reminded of the distance between me and everyone else every day: my body is supposed to be back to normal, but my head hasn't caught up yet. My tumors are gone. Now I'm a cancer survivor. It's supposed to be the end of the story. But will it ever really be over?

Chatting with friends in the pub, voting—for the female candidate perhaps, or maybe the Green Party this time?—meeting new friends, old friends, men. Dating still doesn't come as easily to me as it used to. Whether it's Rob, Jur, Allard, or Tie Boy, it's always complicated. I go through the motions. I get up, pull on my high heels, and stick on my lashes. I get attention easily enough, but that's not what I'm looking for anymore. And love apparently is a whole different matter.

TUESDAY, MAY 20

I stand in front of a very fancy building on the Herengracht. It's one of the mansions built by the nouveau riche of the eighteenth century. Today this neighborhood is home to our mayor, publishing houses, and important lawyers' offices. I ring the bell; the door is opened via the intercom.

"Good morning, I have an appointment with Mr. Spijkers."

"Your name, please?"

"Sophie van der Stap."

"I'll let him know you're here."

The girl behind the reception desk shows me to a waiting area with black leather chairs. I sit down and inspect my surroundings with interest. On the table with newspapers I can see the magazine *NL20*. It's an old edition, the one in which I report on the boat party where everybody was wearing wigs and I left as Cicciolina. Then there are books. A lot of books. I stand up to take a closer look at them.

The hallway is made of white marble and tiles. These traditional Dutch tiles are called *witjes*. I know because my father likes to pass on his historical knowledge about our city everywhere we go. He always has a story, a history, whether we pass gables, street names, or churches. A few months ago we went on a church tour and ended up at one called Ons' Lieve Heer op Solder in the red-light district, hidden in an old, crooked canal house. The secret church is located on the third floor and is fully equipped: organ, balconies, stained-glass windows, and *witjes*. The narrow staircase and numerous visitors made me feel dizzy and tired, so we rested for a while on one of the church pews. Physically, I was a mess. What a difference I feel after only two months.

"Sophie? Follow me, please."

The girl from reception walks ahead of me. She leads me up the imposing staircase, made completely out of marble. She stands still at a high wooden door.

"Sir?"

"Come in!"

She opens the door and leaves me behind. I'm nervous. My hands are sticky, sweaty. Pam suddenly feels kind of warm there on top of my head. The temperature outside has risen to summer levels.

"Welcome, I'm Mai. I'm happy you could make it." After the usual exchange of pleasantries I take a seat. Again, I see books everywhere I look.

"Well, I don't need to say much. We loved your manuscript. It needs a little work here and there, but nothing major. We can publish in the fall. What do you say?"

I look at the man sitting across me. He is as bald as I was a little while back. He has fierce eyes and a big grin on his face. He's dressed elegantly in a crisp white shirt, suspenders, and a tailored suit. Although it's immediately clear that he's the one running the publishing house, there's something relaxed about how he holds himself, with his hands tucked in his pockets. I give him a blank look, at a loss for the right words to say.

"Um, that sounds great."

"Do you have a title?"

"I was thinking *Nine Wigs*."

"*Nine Wigs*," he repeats, shifting sideways in his chair to look out on the canal. *Nine Wigs, Nine Wigs.* He repeats it again several times and looks back at me as if he's a doctor who's examining me. "I like it! It's intriguing. But what about *The Girl with Nine Wigs?*"

I walk home along the canal with a freshly signed contract under my arm. "*The Girl with Nine Wigs* by Sophie van der Stap," it says. It feels kind of super cool, walking home being that girl.

EPILOGUE

It's all real. All the words I've written, all the tears I've cried, all the pain I've faced.

All the nurses, all the IV drips, Dr. L, all the visits to the ER, all the blood transfusions, all the white coats. Dr. K, the vomit buckets, the pills, the tubes, my fake boob, the wet T-shirts, the ladyfingers, the scans, the blood counts, Dr. N, the medical files, all the baldies. My own bald head.

They are all real. Lance, Jur, Oscar, Marco, Chantal.

All the cards, all the phone calls, all the visitors, all the flowers, all the care, all the love, all the sadness, all the worried looks. Those, too, are all real.

Dad, Mom, Sis. So close to me the entire time.

All the meditation attempts, all the organic food shops, all the tomato juice with lemon, all the green tea, all the beetroot, all the seeds and miso soup, a little Jesus. One hundred percent real.

All the wigs, the last hairs I plucked painlessly from my scalp, the last of my pubic hair, which at first I left as some sort of statement but later pulled out. My scars, the destroyed arteries in my right arm, my trusty IV pole, my hospital bed. Real, real, real.

Stella, Daisy, Sue, Blondie, Platina, Uma, Pam, Lydia, Bebé. Real.

And now? I've been given a second chance. It feels so unreal but it's the most real of all. I can't wait to get up and start living again. First destination? Hong Kong.

POSTSCRIPT

Today I'm thirty-two, in good health, and no longer afraid that the cancer will return. All this makes it possible for me to look back at my illness as an experience that I wouldn't have wanted to miss out on. But I don't feel right saying that—cancer is not something to be grateful for. Not ever. The absence of people I dearly loved reminds me of that every day.

Chantal passed away soon after my cancer went into remission, in 2007. It was our cancer that brought us together and connected us until the end. I was in complete awe of her courage facing death. Up until her very last day Chantal was full of joie de vivre and her own incredible sense of humor. She would surprise me with each visit. Either she'd ask about what I had been up to and joke that she had just come back from a long run along the river, or she'd be singing lame Dutch pop music. Even when she was fully paralyzed, she'd always look forward to her bath at six P.M. each evening, which the nurses would fill with rose petals and bath oil. I hated to see her dying; I hated the fact that I had been given a second chance when she hadn't; I hated our cancer. I think I started to hate life, too, when a year later, against all expectations, Jurriaan's cancer returned. He died at the age of twenty-nine. I can't tell you how close to death I felt myself when I lost him. He was such a special and talented person. And also, he still was my dream guy. Some people tried to console me by saying that "God takes the best among us first." That just made me even more angry. Fuck God, was all I could think.

If there's one silver lining to all this suffering, it is that it has brought out a piece of peace in me. My cancer put me more in touch with life. It took away my constant questioning of what life was about and replaced it with the knowledge that life is about love. I have never laughed as wholeheartedly as when I was ill or when sitting next to Chantal's bed in her final days. I don't mean just having a laugh, but those really good belly laughs that bring you to tears and make you feel alive. My illness taught me to embrace life and that actually just means to embrace joy and laughter. Suddenly I had all the time in the world; every minute was mine. I didn't have to waste a single moment on things or people I disliked.

Although cancer takes over your life, we still have the power and ability to turn it into something good—or at least something that is not all bad. This is something that my wigs taught me. They helped me understand that although the cancer was overwhelming, there was still space to create my own parallel reality: in my case, a girl without baggage or drama who just wanted to have some fun. My cancer was always there, when I woke up in the morning, when I fell asleep with tears in my eyes at night. But thanks to my wigs, there were more and more moments when I could say: "Now this is my time, cancer. I'll see you again tonight, but for right now I'm going to go out and live." I truly believe that in the deepest despair we can find refuge and comfort in our minds. Call it escapism or something else; all I know is that it helped me.

This experience taught me to not take things for granted. But now that cancer has become a thing of the past, an experience I survived, I again have days when I struggle with life, days when I take for granted that I walk the planet and forget that once I wasn't even sure I would make it until tomorrow, let alone to age thirty-two. For example, after all I've been through I should celebrate every extra birthday I'm given. But back to the living I'm also back to being a woman who doesn't want to age.

On difficult days, it does help me to think about Jurriaan and Chantal and all the others who were less fortunate than me. Somehow they console me, as much as they did when they were alive. At the very least, I owe them something.

When I think back to what I've gone through, what strikes me most is that my experience is not so much about cancer but about life, and living it. If you change one letter the word "live" becomes "love." If there's any message I'd like to pass on, this is it.

Thank you for reading my story.

Sophie
Paris, June 2015

ACKNOWLEDGMENTS

Ithaka gave you the marvelous journey.
Without her you would not have set out.
She has nothing left to give you now.

—*C. P. Cavafy*

Thank you, Jan, for finding the writer in me. You knew she existed before I did. Thank you, Esther, for developing the writer in me. Thank you, Jaap, for all your literary support. Thank you, Hans, for your crucial advice. Thank you, Walter, for being so much more than my neighbor. Thank you, Jurriaan, for your too short existence. Thank you, Dr. L, for my existence. Thank you, Dr. K, for coloring the hospital for me. Thank you, Dr. N, for your calculations. Thank you Annabel for being the best of friends. Thank you Otto and Bébé for making me feel part of your family. And thank you, Mom, Dad, and Sis, for being my family. Thank you, everyone, for making my story possible.